OUTLAW
JIM
CARTER

OUTLAW JIM CARTER

CLAY WADE - BOOK 5

ART CLEPPER

OUTLAW JIM CARTER
CLAY WADE - BOOK 5

Copyright © 2023 Art Clepper

ISBN: 979-8-9858682-2-7 (sc)
ISBN: 979-8-9858682-3-4 (e)

CHAPTER 1

It was one of those lazy spring days with a slight breeze gently swaying the leaves and giving off a soft hum, and the temperature was near perfect. Laying in the shade, listening to the birds chirp and squirrels bark while chasing each other up and down the trees, seemed the ideal way to start a day. A few lazy clouds drifted by but gave no hint of rain.

Jim Carter had been out since daybreak under the pretense of bagging a fat deer for the kitchen pot, but it looked like they knew he was coming and disappeared into the higher elevations. But today, his mind wasn't on bagging a fat deer.

He had just turned twenty-one a few days back, and Jenny Henry had just turned seventeen. At the dance last night at the schoolhouse, they saw each other for the first time since last fall. He didn't recognize her at first. He thought she was a new girl in the area until she walked up to him and called him by name. When he realized who she was, he couldn't believe his eyes. The last time he saw her, she was a tall skinny little girl, and now she was a full-grown woman. He couldn't keep his eyes from wandering up and down her body.

"Jenny, is that you? What happened to....I mean...you've changed; you're a woman."

She blushed and asked, "You don't like the new me?"

"Well, yeah, I mean, you look so different," his eyes kept wandering over her body.

"Jim, you're embarrassing me. Let's dance, okay?"

He was so surprised it took a while to remember how to dance.

He had been looking at girls for several years but didn't take any of them seriously. His heart was suddenly fluttering and running away at the same time.

After they danced several times, and she got closer each time, she asked him to take a walk to get some fresh air. They left by the front door where everyone could see them leave, but as soon as they were out of sight, she took his hand and led him into the darkness. When they reached the playground, she sat at one of the tables and motioned for him to sit beside her. She was still holding his hand, but she surprised him when she leaned in and kissed him. It was his first kiss, his heart was racing, and he got so dizzy he thought he would pass out as one kiss led to another and another. Both were breathing hard and feeling sensations they had not experienced before, and he wasn't sure how he was supposed to act.

Suddenly she pulled away and said, "We better get back inside before Pa comes looking for us. I'll be at the pool at the waterfall tomorrow morning at about ten. Will you meet me there?"

All he could say was, "Okay."

"So I'll see you there at ten?"

"Huh, yeah, if I can make it."

"You better make it; if you don't, you'll never know what you missed."

He had planned his day to be at the waterfall well before ten. He was biding his time and figured he had another half hour. All kinds of thoughts were running through his mind. If this was what it was like to be in love, he was all in favor of it. He had never felt like this before and didn't know yet if he liked it. But he supposed if he followed his instincts, he would make out okay.

The pond and waterfall were a mile from his home that he shared with his mom and pop since his sister and brother had gone off to Texas with Clay Wade. Clay had been trying to convince them to move to Texas, but since Jenny suddenly became so appealing, he wasn't sure he still wanted to do that.

He checked the sun and decided he should start in that direction. He sure didn't want to be late. His imagination was running wild with pictures of Jenny in the pool, but that was just his wild imagination. He had no idea she would be in the pool as he imagined. But he smiled when that picture flashed through his mind.

He gathered his few things, his rifle, bag of ammunition, and the two squirrels he killed earlier when he gave up on getting a deer and proceeded to the trail that would take him to the pond where Jenny waited.

He was halfway there when he heard what sounded like shots in the distance. Thinking it was probably someone out hunting, he continued toward the pond. The sounds got louder, and there were way too many shots for someone hunting. As he rounded the end of the hill separating him from his home range, the shots became much clearer and sounded much closer. He stopped to listen again and became worried. That sounded like it was coming from the direction of his home. His mom and pop were there alone. Racing as fast as his legs could carry him, he reached the top of the hill overlooking the home place. He was still half a mile away when he saw smoke billowing toward the sky and men on horses racing about the place firing their weapons. The house and barn were in flames, and there was no sign of his parents.

The rifle he had with him would be useless at that distance, and he was sitting on the edge of a cliff overlooking his home, but to get there, he would have to run a half mile to the nearest trail off the cliff, then another half mile back. He knew he would be too late to do any good, so in desperation, he raised the rifle and aimed at the nearest rider, knowing it was hopeless, but he was desperate. He elevated the sights to allow for the excessive distance, hoping he could scare them away before they could do more damage. He pulled the trigger, levered another round into the chamber, and fired again and again until the rifle was empty. He was surprised and satisfied when one of the riders dropped his gun and fell from his horse. The rest of the men, seeing one of theirs fall to gunfire from such a distance, decided it was time to leave. They raced away to the east, leaving a cloud of dust in their wake.

Jim raced down the hill. When he reached the house, all out of breath, all the buildings, even the outhouse, were in flames. The fire was too hot to get close to any of them. Frantically, he raced around the grounds looking for his parents. He called out repeatedly, but the only sound he heard was the crackling of the fire and the death bells ringing in his ears. All he could do was stand and watch everything he had grown up with slowly crumble. He dropped to his knees and cried while watching his life go up in smoke.

He kept looking toward the trees and brush, calling for his mom and dad, hoping to see them walking toward him. But he could only imagine what had happened to them.

After what seemed like hours, he got to his feet and walked around the pile of ashes, looking for some sign of his parents. He was still carrying the empty rifle that would be of no use to him if the culprits returned, but just having it in his hands gave him some comfort.

During his walk, he spotted the body of the man he had shot from the top of the cliff. With his foot, he turned it over to get a look at his face to see what kind of man could do this. A bullet hole in the left temple had killed him instantly. After thinking about it, he wished he had shot him in the gut so he would suffer for hours before he died.

He was still in a daze when he heard horses galloping toward him. Realizing his rifle was empty and he had no other weapon, he turned to face four riders as they raced into the yard and pulled their horses to a halt in front of Jim. He was too stunned to do anything but stare at them.

One of the riders jumped to the ground, ran to Jim, and threw her arms around his neck. "Oh, Jim, are you okay? What happened? Are you okay? I heard the shots, and when you didn't come, I knew something bad had happened."

Jenny was there. He dropped the rifle, and his arms encircled her body, holding on for dear life. They were both shaking and crying and mumbling unintelligible words that neither of them would remember later.

Jenny's dad came forward after looking around to discover what he could. "Jim, do you know who did this or why?"

Jim pulled himself together, wiped his eyes and nose on his shirt sleeve, and shook his head no. "I was over the hill hunting and heard the shots, and by the time I got here, the place was in flames. I got one of the sorry bastards, though," as he pointed to the body.

"Well, that's something. Maybe it'll give us a clue to go on."

They walked to the body and examined it to see what they could learn. He was wearing the remains of a confederate uniform, which didn't say much since hundreds, maybe thousands of former union and confederates roamed the country with no place to call home. Gangs rode through the countryside, taking everything they could get their hands on at the expense of anyone who got in their way.

Jenny's father put his arms around Jim's shoulders and said, "Jim, there's nothing we can do here until the fire burns out. Come home with us, and we'll come back tomorrow and try to sort things out."

Jim was still in shock and unable to decide anything for himself, so he allowed Jenny and her dad to lead him away. He kept looking back, hoping to see his mom and dad, but that was not to be.

One of the men caught a horse from a nearby pasture and brought it to Jim. All the saddles and riding gear had burned, so he mounted bareback and rode away in a trance.

Mrs. Henry prepared a nice meal, but he was in no mood to eat. He drank a lemonade but didn't even realize what he was drinking. When it was time for bed, Jenny showed him to his room. He fell across the bed, but his mind was in too much turmoil to sleep.

Jenny removed his boots, lay beside him, and tried to console him. All he could see and think about was his parents in the smoldering fire of his home that didn't exist anymore.

The night passed slowly, filled with one nightmare after another. He woke up fighting several times, and Jenny held him until it passed. When morning finally came, he was too tired to get out of bed, but he knew he must.

During the night, when he had wild dreams, he decided to track down the killers and see them pay for their crime if it took the rest of his life.

He dragged himself out of bed and into the kitchen to eat breakfast with Jenny and her family. He had no appetite but knew he had to eat, so he forced it down until he could hold no more.

Mr. Henry and three of his men accompanied Jim when they returned to the crime scene. Jenny went along to be a comfort to Jim and never left his side. When they arrived, the ashes were still smoking, but nothing was left to salvage. They poked through the ashes and debris until they found the bodies of his mom and dad in the corner of the bedroom where they had put up their last fight.

The remains were removed and buried in the family cemetery that contained his mom's parents and a headstone for his sister Ellen, but she wasn't there. She was buried in Texas at her home near Cuero, where she met her death.

After the burial, Jim asked those gathered to give him some time to himself. He had things to think about and decisions to make. They honored his request and departed, leaving him alone.

He sat on the ground at the foot of the graves and said farewell to his parents. He didn't know what to say, so he sat remembering all the happy times that took place here. He looked around at the grounds, the trees, and all the hiding places they took advantage of when he and his brother and sister were small.

When he could think of nothing else, he mounted his horse and rode to the top of the hill where he was when his life went up in smoke. He dismounted, tied his horse, sat in the shade of a tall pine tree, and looked down on his home. He was picturing the scene as it was when he last saw it.

The buildings were burning, and men were racing about firing at the house. As he sat there, things began to become clearer to him. One of the men was riding a black horse with four white stockings; another was riding a gray with a black mane and tail. The others were just dim images that he couldn't put together.

For over an hour, he sat and reviewed what he knew and could remember. Those two horses would be enough to lead him to the murderers. If they stayed together, he would find them, and they would regret this day when he did.

Then he began thinking about how to carry out his plan. First, he needed money. With the money, he could buy the necessary supplies for his search. There were horses and cattle on the farm that he could sell if he could find a buyer, but he didn't have much time to look for one.

When he had thought everything through, he got on his horse, trailing a second horse, and rode to the Henry home to tell them he was leaving. They didn't like it, but his mind was made up, and there was no changing it.

Jenny was crying and begging him not to go, but he forced himself to stick to his plan. He promised to return for her when he finished the job he had to do if she was still there. She promised she would wait for him no matter how long it took.

She stood in the front yard crying and waved to him as he rode away.

His first stop was at Sheriff Campbell's office in Rogersville, where he reported the murders and fire. His next stop was the bank where his folks did their banking. After some convincing, he got the banker to make a loan against the property and livestock. "If I don't come back, you can sell the place to get your money."

With the money in his pocket, he purchased a used saddle, a pack-saddle, and enough supplies to last him a month. He hoped that would be enough time to complete the job.

During his conversation with the sheriff, he described the two horses and inquired if he had seen them. "No, I ain't seen 'em, but now that I know what to look for, I'll be on the lookout."

With everything taken care of that he could think to do, he stopped at the train depot and sent a telegram to his brother Ed in the care of the sheriff in Cuero, Texas.

"Mom and Dad dead, place burned, I'm on their trail, Jim."

He looked at the town where he had attended school, danced, played, fought with the local kids, and danced with Jenny just a few days ago. He rode out of town with tears streaming down his face, not knowing if he would ever see it, or any of his friends, again.

Since, according to Sheriff Campbell, the gang had not come through Rogersville, the only logical route was east. If that's where they went, his work was cut out for him. There were hundreds of trails through those mountains where a gang of men could easily get lost.

He returned to the home place and picked up their trail. The tracks were not hard to follow. They were the freshest ones going in the right direction. He took his time and studied the prints trying to distinguish some differences that would stand out. At first, nothing jumped out at him, but after following them for a mile or so, he noticed that one of the horses looked like he had a loose shoe. He got down and looked closer and believed he was right. If that were true, that horse would be lame before very long. The shoe would eventually fall off or get so loose the horse would favor that hoof. So, knowing that, he began thinking about where the next blacksmith shop was. He was not too familiar with the towns in this direction, so all he could do for now was follow the tracks and hope they stopped somewhere soon.

He started two days behind, so there didn't seem to be a need to hurry too much. He could wear his horses out or take his time and plan on the long haul.

Late in the afternoon, he came to the first settlement. The usual saloon, general store, blacksmith/livery stable, and a few other mom-and-pop stores lined the streets.

He rode through the town, looking at every horse along the way. On the way back, he stopped at the livery and walked through. The proprietor asked if he could help him.

"I'm looking for a group of men who rode through here sometime during the last two days. One was riding a black with four stockings, and another was riding a gray with a black mane and tail. One of the horses had a loose shoe. Did you see them come through here?"

"Why are you looking for them?"

"They killed my mom and pop and burned our place to the ground two days ago. I've tracked them here. Now have you seen them or not?"

"Yeah, they were here, and as you said, one of them had a loose shoe. I took care of the horse, and they went on their way."

"When was that?"

"That was the day before yesterday, late in the evening; I was just closing up to go to supper when they rode in. I couldn't get rid of them fast enough. That was the meanest bunch I ever saw. They were in a hurry to be on the way, and I helped them as fast as I could. I wanted them out of here as bad as they wanted out."

"Did you see where they went when they left here?"

"Yeah, there were five of them. Four went to the saloon while the other waited here while I worked on his horse."

"Did you see them when they left town?"

"No, I went home to supper and didn't come out until the next morning."

"Can you describe them to me? I never saw any of them up close. The two horses are the only thing I have to go by."

"They were just a bunch of dirty, ragged ex-confederates from the looks of their uniforms. Most had beards and long dirty hair."

"What about the other horses? What did they look like?"

"The black and gray were the only two that stood out. The others were sorrels and bays, nothing unusual about them."

Jim thought for a minute, and when he had no more questions, he thanked the man for his help and left to go to the saloon. When he walked in, everyone turned to look at him. There weren't but six men in the place, counting the bartender, and one woman who looked like she should go home and sleep for two days.

When his eyes had adjusted to the dim interior, he made his way to the bar that ran along the right side, from front to rear. A fly-specked mirror hung on the wall behind the bar with a shelf lined with whiskey bottles in front of it, giving the impression of two rows of bottles.

Jim removed his hat and placed it on the bar before him. The bartender put down the rag he was using to polish glasses and asked him what he would have.

"I'll have a beer, please."

A snicker behind him caused him to look in the mirror to see where it came from. Three men who looked like cowhands sat at one table, looking at him and laughing. Jim ignored them until one of them said, "Did you hear that 'I'll have a beer, please?'" They all snickered again and looked at Jim.

Jim was not a big man, but he was built solid and carried himself like he would be a handful in a rough-and-tumble fight. He stood five feet eight inches and weighed one hundred eighty-five pounds. Broad through the shoulders, thick through the chest, and his arms bulged with muscle. His legs stretched his pant legs tight, and his waist was small, making everything else look larger.

An unruly mop of curly reddish-blond hair covered his head. But his most striking feature was his bright blue eyes.

He ignored the snickers until one of them said, "Hey, Red, don't you think you ought to be drinking milk instead of beer?"

Knowing things would worsen if he continued to ignore them, he turned his back to the bar, rested both elbows on it, and looked the three over. They covered their mouths and laughed. Jim stared at them and didn't speak for the longest time. When the man realized he was not going to take the bait, the one with the mouth stood up and approached the bar, "Hey, Sam, give the boy a soda pop. He can't handle a man's drink."

The man was probably in his late twenties or early thirties, six feet tall, and two hundred pounds. The way he pushed his weight around, he must have thought he was the bull of the woods around here.

The bartender paid no attention to his demands except to tell him, "Leave the man alone, Tim. Go back and sit down. This man has done nothing to bother you."

"You mind your own business, Sam. I'm talking to this kid. Now give the boy his soda pop."

Jim turned around, facing the bar with the bully on his right, "Make that two soda pops, Barkeep. I hate to drink alone."

The barkeep gave him a sharp look, picked up two soda pop bottles, and popped the caps. "Okay," he whispered, "It's your funeral."

Jim pushed one bottle toward the loudmouth, "Here, drink up. You're the one who suggested the soda pop. I think it'll fit your style."

"Why, you smart-mouth punk. I'll teach you about style."

He was turning toward Jim with his fist drawn back, ready to strike, when the pop bottle caught him in the mouth. Jim had backhanded it with all his strength. Tim staggered back, tripped over a chair, then a table, and ended up on his back with his feet in the air over the table. He was so stunned he couldn't move for almost a minute. When he realized where he was and what had happened, he roared like a bull, came off the floor, and attempted to charge Jim, but he was so unsteady on his feet that he fell twice before maintaining his footing. When he finally was steady enough to make his way toward Jim, he was weaving unsteadily, and when he swung a fist, Jim easily ducked it and landed a solid left hook to his stomach. Tim staggered back, sat on the floor, and threw up the contents of his stomach all over his clothes.

Jim calmly took a sip of his soda pop, smacked his lips, and said, "That's not bad. Come on, Tim, you don't know what you're missing.

This will probably stay on your stomach better than the beer you've been drinking."

The two friends at the table were in shock. One of them looked Jim up and down and said, "Look, Kid, you better get out of here while you can. He'll tear you apart limb by limb when he comes to his senses."

"From what I've seen, he can't control his own limbs; how is he going to do anything with mine?"

"You've been lucky so far. Leave while you're ahead."

"I didn't come in here looking for trouble; he's the one who started it, and it looks like he's not big enough to back up his big mouth."

"Like I said, Kid, leave while you're ahead."

"Okay, I'll be going, but y'all just remember, he started this, not me."

Then he remembered what he came here for in the first place. "By the way, I came here looking for five men, dirty confederate uniforms, one riding a black with four stockings and a gray with black mane and tail. Y'all see them around here the last couple of days?"

He kept an eye on Tim and his two friends, not knowing if they might suddenly decide to participate in the ruckus.

The Bartender, Sam, said, "Yeah, there were some men in here the day before yesterday about sundown. They had a few drinks and left. They looked like they could be a world of trouble. Why are you looking for them? You don't look like their type."

Jim explained why he was looking for them and asked, "Which way did they go when they left?"

"It was dark, and the place was pretty busy. I didn't see which way they went. Take my advice and don't find them. They are nothing but trouble."

Jim took the last swig of his beer, looked down at Tim sitting on the floor holding his head, with blood dripping from his nose and mouth, and left the saloon.

As he was riding out of town, he saw a café and thought this might be his last chance for a good meal for a long time. He tied his horses in front, went in, and enjoyed a good meal.

CHAPTER 2

The road out of town to the east took him down a steep hill and around a sharp bend to a swift-running stream with a small waterfall just up from the crossing. He had traveled about as far as he wanted to for one day, so he found a small clearing on the bank of the stream and pitched his bedroll. There was plenty of grass, so the horses had their fill during the night while he slept.

He was so tired and unused to spending the entire day in the saddle that he slept the night through. He was surprised when he awoke, and the sun was almost up. With nothing else to do, he saddled his horse, packed his supplies on the packsaddle, and returned to the trail to see if he could find the tracks of the five men.

After a short search, he found where they crossed the stream and continued east. He picked up the pace and intended to maintain that speed for most of the day.

He had only gone about ten miles up the trail from the little town where he fought with Tim when he heard a group of horses coming fast on the trail behind him. Something told him this was not a good sign, so he moved off the trail into the thick brush at the first opportunity and waited for them to pass. Six men, led by a man wearing a badge, raced by and continued along the trail. The more he sat and thought about what he saw, the more uneasy he became. Those men were looking for someone and looked like they had fire in their eyes. He didn't know what or who they were after, but he didn't like the feeling in his bones.

He had no reason to think they were looking for him, but he couldn't ignore the bells going off in his head. He sat his horse thinking about it and decided to play it safe and assume the worst.

He waited until he couldn't hear them, then he crossed the trail and followed the base of the hill that had him going northeast. He had no idea where this would take him, but he knew he didn't want to be where that posse was. The more he thought about it, the more worried he became. What happened back there to put the law on his trail, if they were even after him? He didn't know, but he wasn't taking any chances. He would avoid contact with them and stay out of trouble.

Then the thought occurred to him that maybe they were after the same men he was after, but after some thought, he didn't want to take the chance that he was wrong.

He followed the bottom of the hill, bringing him back to a more easterly direction and eventually southeast. He knew he was losing valuable time and distance to the killers, but he couldn't help it, and that posse worried him.

If he kept going in this direction, he would end up back in the vicinity of the original trail where he first saw the posse. He didn't know if that was a good thing or not. He didn't want to run into them again, but he didn't want to lose the killers' trail either. So he continued following the contour of the hills and hoped things turned out for the best.

Late that day, he intersected a road that looked like it had a lot of use, similar to the original road he was on when he encountered the posse. He dismounted and walked along the road looking for tracks that he recognized. He wasn't sure, but he thought he saw some that looked familiar. The problem was they were ridden over by another set of tracks, probably made by the posse.

Wouldn't it be something if the posse was after the same gang he was after? That was asking for too much luck, so he didn't put much hope on that.

For the rest of the day, he followed the tracks but was always alert that he may encounter the posse coming back. Whenever he saw or heard riders coming, he got off the trail as fast as possible and hid in the brush or rocks until they passed. So far, none of them had been members of the posse.

Late in the day, he came to the outskirts of a small settlement on the edge of a valley surrounded by mountains on all sides. He had never seen a prettier sight in his short life. Everything was green, with flowers scattered over the valley floor and a stream running through the middle. The mountains were not so steep that cattle and horses could graze the slopes. Everywhere he looked was so peaceful it made him wonder why anyone would want to live anywhere else.

He looked over the valley a long time before he descended the trail that took him into the town. Before he reached the lower level, he saw where the road continued out the other side of town and climbed the mountain, so he skirted the town on the south side and intersected the road on the other side. After a short search, he found the tracks of the killers. The five killers had come this way not too long ago. The tracks were much fresher than the last ones he saw. They must have spent the night in town and left early this morning. More searching did not reveal the posse tracks, so he assumed they were still in town. He picked up the pace and made good time for several hours until his horses needed to stop for a rest. It was time to start looking for a place to spend the night. Good camping spots were not hard to find. The terrain was very hilly, with a stream at the bottom of each hill with grass very thick along its banks.

Shortly after sundown, he rode off the trail, following one of the small streams for half a mile until he found a good spot. It only took a few minutes to stake his horses on the grass near the water and get a fire going.

Supper was very sparse, consisting of coffee, jerky, and a cold biscuit from his last meal with Jenny.

Just the thought of Jenny made him have second thoughts about his mission. Back there was everything a man could want: a beautiful girl and a home, but he would have to rebuild if he stayed in the home place since there was nothing left except the livestock. He could probably sell enough cattle to get the money to build a nice house for Jenny.

The more he thought about it, the more he realized he should turn back and give up trying to find the killers. But he couldn't do it when he thought about them getting away scot-free. With added determination, he concentrated on the job at hand. Tomorrow he would continue his search in earnest.

He removed all the wood from the fire to let it die down. He didn't want to send up smoke signals or leave the fire burning to draw anyone to him while he slept.

It took a long time to get to sleep, but when he did, he slept well. He was tired from being in the saddle all day, but when morning came, he was up early, reheated the coffee from last night, and chewed on a stick of jerky while he saddled his horse and packed his gear.

As he left his camp to take up the trail, both horses threw up their heads, with ears pointed toward the trail. Jim slid off his horse and put his hand over their nose to keep them quiet. The riders were moving faster than your casual traveler, so he waited until they were out of hearing distance and then led his horses out to the road to inspect the tracks. He found what he was hoping to avoid. He was sure these were the tracks of the posse. He still had no reason to believe they were after him, but he had a bad feeling. Something wasn't right.

That put a whole new light on the subject. He didn't feel safe following in the posse tracks, but he didn't want to lose the trail of the killers either. But, when he weighed one against the other, he chose to temporarily lose the killers' tracks against being apprehended by the posse. With that decision, he searched for another way through the mountains to the northeast. That's the direction everyone seemed to be headed. There weren't too many choices when it came to picking a trail. The mountains were too steep for a horse to climb in most places, so he followed the streams and tried to stay as close to the northeast direction as he could, which wasn't easy. The terrain dictated where he could ride.

He saw some of the most beautiful country but was too worried to appreciate it. The high mountains covered with giant pine trees, water seeping from the rocks, and meandering down the slopes created a scene he never wanted to forget.

He thought that Jenny would love the beauty of this place. If he ever got the chance, he would bring her here when his death search was over if he survived.

He was following the winding course of Holston River, which was taking him northeast and would take him into Virginia if he didn't catch up with his prey before they got there, which didn't look likely.

There were several small settlements along the way, and he checked the trails leading into them before he entered the towns. A ride up and down the main street usually told him all he needed to know. When he didn't see the killer's horses or the horses belonging to the posse, he stopped at the first saloon to inquire. So far, no one had seen anyone fitting their description. Most small settlements only had one saloon, so it didn't take long to make his inquiries.

About noon on the third day out, he rode into the town of Kingsport, just south of the Virginia state line. All the roads and trails leading into town were too well-traveled to make out any tracks, so he took his chances and rode in.

Kingsport was the busiest town he had ever seen. Sidewalks crowded with people rushed to do their shopping or whatever their business was.

He pulled his hat low over his forehead and kept his head down as he slowly rode from one end of town to the other and back again. On the way back, he stopped at each livery stable and strolled through and out the back door to check the corrals in the back. By the time he reached the opposite end of town and found no trace of the killers or the posse, he was ready to find something to eat. He was so hungry it didn't matter what, he just wanted something other than jerky to put in his stomach.

The first café he saw looked good enough from the outside, so he scraped his boots on the steps, pushed the door open, removed his hat, and stepped inside. It took a moment for his eyes to adjust to the dim interior. He quickly took in the other diners, who only gave him a passing glance and went about their business of eating. None of them looked to be a threat, so he took a seat at a table near the back door in case he decided to leave in a hurry.

A very pretty young woman, who couldn't have been older than sixteen or seventeen, came to take his order. When he looked into her eyes, his heart skipped a beat, and he had trouble concentrating on the menu. She smiled as she waited for him to make his selection. His mind was not on the menu but on the waitress. Finally, she said, "The special today is beef stew, with lots of potatoes, carrots, celery, and everything else in the kitchen."

"Okay, that sounds perfect; bring me a big serving of that, a pot of coffee, and cornbread."

"Coming right up. Would you like your coffee now?"

"Yes, thank you. By the way, may I ask you a question?"

"Sure."

In a voice just above a whisper, he described the men, and before he finished with the description, her face turned white, and she started shaking. He thought she would faint before she sat down in the nearest chair.

"I take it they were here."

"Yes, they were here and caused a lot of trouble. They killed two men at the saloon before they finally left town."

"When did this happen?"

"Last night. They came in here after spending several hours drinking and causing trouble. If Ma didn't have her shotgun under the counter and threatened to use it, there's no telling what they would have done."

"Did they hurt you?"

"No, they threatened to take me with them, but Ma's sawed-off 12-gauge changed their minds quickly."

"You don't know how lucky you are."

"What do you mean, do you know those men?"

"I don't know them, but I know their kind. I'm after them for killing my ma and pa and burning our place to the ground a couple of days back."

"Oh, that's awful. I'm so sorry."

"Thank you."

"I'll get your food."

"Take your time."

The food came, and he ate like a starved man until it was all gone and then sat back and stretched while the waitress refilled his coffee cup.

While she poured the coffee, he asked her, "Have you seen them again since your mom ran them out of here last night?"

"No, but they caused a ruckus at the saloon last night and killed two men."

"Were they local men, or was it two of the bad men?"

"It was two local hands from one of the ranches."

"What did the law do about it?"

"What law? Our sheriff is scared of his own shadow. He runs and hides if he hears a shot and says he didn't hear anything."

The more they talked, the more intrigued he became. "What is your name?"

"I'm Lacy Malone, my mom owns this café, and my dad owns the hardware store across the street."

"I'm glad to meet you, Lacy; I'm Jim Carter, from over near Rogersville. I've been following those men for the last three days. This is the closest I've been. I wonder if they are still around."

"I sure hope not. I don't ever want to see them again."

"I don't blame you, but I want to catch them before they hurt anyone else."

"What do you plan to do when you catch them?"

"I don't know. I guess I haven't thought it through that far."

"Well, I hope you never catch them. They are evil men. I hate to think about what might happen if you catch them."

"I don't think about that part. I only think about what I want to do to them."

"Look, why don't you ask around town? The men who were killed had friends. Maybe they will join you. It'll be a lot safer for everyone."

"I'll ask around. Which ranch did those boys work for?"

"I heard they were both from Ward Parker's ranch."

"Thanks, I better get going. Maybe I'll see you again if I come this way."

"I'll be here. Be careful and good luck."

Jim left the café and went to the saloon where the two men were killed. When he pushed his way through the bat-wing doors, everyone turned to look his way. The light inside was so dim that he couldn't see anything for a minute, so he stood inside the door until his eyes adjusted. About six or eight men sat at tables and stood at the bar, but none looked like the ones he was after. A couple of girls were hanging around talking to the men, but they didn't seem interested in what the girls were selling.

It was a typical saloon with a bar running along the wall on the left side. A door at the far end of the bar led to the privy out back and maybe to some private rooms that were rented by the hour. A painting of a mostly nude woman hung over the bar with several bullet holes that missed the target.

Jim walked to the bar and ordered a beer. The bartender drew the beer, sat it before him, and waited while Jim fished out a nickel to pay for it. He took a long swig and smacked his lips. No one had said a word since he entered the door. When he realized that, he looked around the room, and everyone was looking at him.

"What's going on? Why is everyone staring at me?"

The bartender asked, "Did you ride in from the west?"

"Yeah, I did. Why?"

"There was a sheriff's posse here early this morning looking for a man that fits your description."

"Oh," as chills ran up and down his back, "and what did the sheriff want this man for?"

"He said you killed a man in Surgoinsville yesterday, and you're wanted for his murder."

There was a commotion behind Jim, and before he could react, two men grabbed him and pinned his arms behind his back while a third man took his revolver.

"Hey, wait a minute, I didn't kill anyone. I came here looking for five men who killed my mom and dad and burned our place to the ground three days ago. I heard two men were killed here last night, and I was hoping I could get some help tracking them down. But I sure as hell didn't kill anybody."

"That's not what the sheriff said."

"What makes you think he was looking for me? Did he give my name or have a wanted poster on me or anything else that makes you think I'm the one he was looking for?"

"You fit the description. That's good enough for us."

"My description could fit half the men in this town."

"That may be so, but we know the men in this town, and we don't know you."

"That's not good enough. You got to have more proof than that."

Jim was struggling with the men holding him, trying to break free. Another man stepped in front of him at said, "Hold him. I'll quiet him down." He drew back his fist to punch Jim in the face, but before he could let fly with the fist, Jim brought both feet up and kicked the man in the face sending him flying across the room. As Jim's feet hit the floor, he bent forward at the waist and jerked both arms forward, sending both men flying to meet the man he had just kicked in the face. The three collided in a pile, and before they could gain their feet, Jim was holding a six-shooter. They made a mistake putting his pistol on the bar within his reach.

"Now, just calm down before some of you get shot."

From the corner of his eye, Jim saw the bartender reaching under the bar. With the hammer clicking back to full cock, Jim brought his gun around, "I wouldn't do that unless you're ready to die. Get your hands where I can see them, and move down to that end of the bar."

When Barkeep was standing at the other end, Jim walked around behind the bar and picked up a sawed-off shotgun, broke it open, saw it was loaded, snapped it closed, dropped his revolver in his holster, and held the shotgun.

"As you might guess, I'm not in a very friendly mood right now, so don't push me. For your information, I didn't kill anybody anywhere, so don't make me start here. Like I said, I came here looking for help to track down the men who killed my ma and pa. I think the same men killed the two men here last night. But since y'all are so anxious to hang an innocent man, I don't suppose any of you would want to go after five guilty men, would you?"

When no one answered, he said, "That's what I figured, just a bunch of gutless wonders that will gang up on one man but don't have the guts to go after the gang that killed your friends. So forget about helping me. I wouldn't trust any of you to ride with me."

He pointed to the man who had done all the talking, "You are coming with me. I'm going to get my horse and ride out of town. If anybody tries to follow me, this man will pay the price. Come on, let's go."

The man struggled to his feet and timidly walked ahead of Jim as they left the saloon. Jim watched his back as he marched the man down the street until he reached his horses in front of the café. Keeping the horse between them, he mounted and told the man to walk in front of him. He led the man to the edge of town, where he repeated, "I didn't kill anyone. I don't know why you're so fired up to kill me, but take my advice and forget about it. If I see any of you coming after me, I'll shoot to kill, and you will be the first one I shoot. Have you got that?"

The man stood staring at him while Jim broke open the shotgun, removed the two loads, tossed the gun to the man, turned his horse, and rode away. Jim wanted to get much rougher with the man but decided to leave well enough alone. Maybe they would believe him and forget about trying to catch him.

He put the spurs to his horse and left Kingsport. After a mile of fast riding, he pulled his horse down to a trot and started looking for a place to get off this main road. All the time, he watched his back trail for any sign that he was being followed. So far, he had not seen any dust back there, but the road was so crooked he couldn't be sure where it was after so many twists and turns.

After another mile, a small river, or creek, came cascading down the side of the mountain and cut across the road. He stopped in the water so his horse wouldn't leave tracks and looked both ways, up and down the creek, to decide which way he wanted to go. The water flowed to his right, which would be to the south; the other way would be higher in the mountains and harder to travel. The logical direction would be south, which looked like the much easier route, so he turned north to make for the high country. Anyone following him would have their work cut out for them.

He followed the stream for the rest of the day, which sometimes was not easy. Waterfalls and boulders blocked the way, and at times the climb was so steep he had to get down and lead his horses. By sundown, his horses were ready for a rest. Another small stream came in from the left, so he turned up it, still riding in the water where he would leave no trail. A mile later, he came to an opening on the creek bank and stopped to camp for the night.

His horses were stripped of their gear and staked on the grass at the creek's edge. He didn't want to have a fire and lead any followers directly to him, but he had to have food, and he desperately needed his coffee. He got a fire going, made a small pot of coffee, heated some beans, and ate them right out of the can. As soon as the coffee was ready, he pulled the sticks back from the fire and let it die down to just a bed of coals while he ate the beans and drank his coffee. By the time he finished eating, he was ready to turn in.

Now that he had time to think over what had happened during the day, he was more confused than ever. It appeared that he was now a wanted man. Then he thought about the fight with the man named Tim. Did he die after he left town? He didn't know he hit him hard enough to kill him. He had hit other men harder, and they bounced right back, so he couldn't believe that's who he was accused of killing.

His mind was a jumble of thoughts until he finally fell into a restless sleep. He tossed and turned all night and dreamed of men chasing him, and at one time, they had a rope around his neck when he lunged out of his blanket, ready to fight. His revolver was in his hand, and he was look-ing for someone to shoot when he awoke and realized where he was. The rest of the night was a blur of bad dreams mixed with the pretty face of Jenny floating in and out.

When morning came, he was a wreck. He was more tired than when he went to bed, but he knew he had to get up and move. The men he was after were getting farther ahead, and the sheriff's posse may be getting closer. Should he keep moving and leave tracks that anyone could follow, or should he lay up somewhere and let the posse wear themselves out look-ing for him where he wasn't? If he left no tracks, no one could trail him. On the other hand, they may already know right where he was.

With that thought, he looked around, expecting men to come out of the brush with guns blazing. His horses were grazing contentedly, so he relaxed, got his fire from last night stirred up, put the coffee pot on, and opened a can of peaches from his pack. That and a strip of jerky made his breakfast. By then, he had decided to stay right where he was and see what happened. He was satisfied with how he hid his trail yesterday, so he didn't think anyone would be able to follow him.

He moved his horses to new grass so they would have plenty to eat for several more hours, took his rifle and binoculars, and walked down the creek toward where it flowed into the larger tributary. From a spot high on a hill overlooking the junction of the two streams, he sat down to spend the day or until someone came along to change his mind.

CHAPTER 3

He sat in the shade, dozed off and on, chewed on jerky, and drank from his canteen until he couldn't stand it anymore. He hadn't seen nor heard anyone all day, so he was pleased with his decision to sit it out and let the posse wear out their horses and men. But, after a day of lying around doing nothing, he didn't know how long he could do this. In his twenty-one years, he had never had a day where he didn't have something to do. There was always something that needed doing, whether splitting wood for the kitchen stove, checking on the cattle, or repairing a fence. Hundreds of little jobs could keep a man busy if he was willing to do the work.

By the middle of the third day, he had all he could take of doing nothing. He brought his horses in, saddled one, put the pack on the other, snuffed out his small fire, and did everything he could to erase all sign that he had been here.

He mounted his horse, rode down the creek to where it intersected the larger one, and waited a few minutes before riding into the open water. Instead of going back the way he came, he turned to the right and went in the opposite direction. He didn't know where this would come out, but he didn't want to return to where he knew the posse was looking for him.

He had one thing in his favor. The state line of Virginia was somewhere ahead. That would be out of the sheriff's jurisdiction, so he hoped he didn't run into him before he left Tennessee.

He kept plodding along, following the most accessible route through the hills and streams, trying to keep heading as close to the northeast as possible. Somewhere ahead, he expected to come to a town. There he could learn if he was still in Tennessee or if he was in Virginia.

For the first two hours, he kept his horses in the water where that was possible. Finally, deciding he was far enough from where he was last seen, he was willing to take his chances on dry land. His horses were tired from fighting the current and rocks on the river bottom. They both took a deep breath when he rode out of the water and broke into a trot.

When night came, he still had not come to a road or town, so he made camp on the bank of the stream and turned in. His supper consisted of coffee and jerky. He was so tired of that diet he was ready to shoot some fresh meat, but with a posse on his trail, he was holding off as long as he could.

Early the following day, he heard noises up the river as he was breaking camp. He listened until he thought he recognized what it was. A few minutes later, when he rounded a curve, he saw a house and barns sitting on the hill above the river.

He sat on his horse and watched the house for a few minutes. A man came from the barn carrying a bucket. He assumed he had just milked his cow and was taking the fresh milk to the house. Everything looked normal, so he rode into the open and stopped about twenty feet from the front door. "Hello, the house. Is anyone home?" He sat with his hands in sight on the horn of his saddle and waited until the man came out the front door.

"Can I help you?"

"I was passing by and wanted to ask a few questions. I'm new to this part of the country and need to get some direction. Am I still in Tennessee?"

"No, if you came up the road, you've been in Virginia for the last hour or so."

"I knew the line was somewhere around here, but I didn't see a sign. How far is it to the next town?"

"Weber City is just up the road apiece."

"I'm trailing five men who may have come by here a few days back. They were all dressed in remnants of confederate uniforms, one was riding a black horse with four stockings, and another one was riding a gray with a black mane and tail. Have you seen anyone fitting that description?"

"No, I didn't see them, but I heard talk about a shooting in Weber. It sounds like the same men. They are supposed to have robbed the bank and killed everyone in it. Why are you looking for them? Are you the law?" Jim told the story of the raid on their homestead.

"Well, I hope you catch 'em. We got no use for scum like that."

"When did this robbery take place?"

"That was just yesterday. The neighbor over there was in town then and saw the whole thing."

"Thanks, I'll be on my way." He tipped his hat and rode on toward Weber City.

As he rode, he removed his hat and scratched his head, "Still a whole day behind. They must have held up for a few days like I did, or I would be farther behind." He picked up the pace and made it into Weber City before nightfall. It looked like the typical little town with saloons outnumbering the rest of the business. Jim had never spent much time in town, so he had very little experience with saloons, but he knew that was the place to get information. But then he remembered the last saloon where he got in the fight with Tim and may have killed him if the story the sheriff was spreading was true.

The general store was open, so he stopped there first and replenished his supplies. The owner there had heard about the robbery and shooting, but what he knew was only hearsay. Jim stashed his food in his pack, walked his horses down to the first saloon, and stepped up to the bar.

"What'll it be, stranger?"

"How about a beer?"

"Coming right up, are you just passing through, or will you be around for a while?"

"I guess that depends on what information I can get."

"What kind of information are you looking for?"

"Information on the robbery and killing that took place yesterday. I think I'm looking for those same men for another killing."

"Well, you're a day late, friend. They were here and killed some good people and left a lot of others with their life savings gone."

"Did anyone see which way they went when they left here?"

"According to the sheriff, they went north, but no one has seen them since they tore out of here with everyone's money."

Jim took his time sipping his beer and enjoying being out of the saddle. He had a second beer for the first time in his life and then rode out of town. He stopped and made camp for the night a mile up the road.

When he finished his meal, and the fire was down to a small bed of coal, he leaned back against his saddle and enjoyed a last cup of coffee before turning in.

The sun was down, the stars were out, coyotes were barking in the distance, and the wind picked up as the temperature dropped. He tried to relax, but his mind kept wandering back to Jenny. He thought he could be back there enjoying a quiet, peaceful life, but instead, he was alone in the dark woods, chasing after the men who murdered his parents and no telling how many others. Was it his job to track them down and bring them to justice? He didn't know the answer to that. But if he didn't, then who would?" He didn't know the answer to that either.

The wind picked up, and the air felt damp. Black clouds swirled above, and stars were only visible far away to the east. The sky to the west and north was black. Lightning flashed, and thunder rumbled far away. He realized he was going to be in for a wet night. All he had for protection against such a night was a ground sheet and a small one-person tent. He got busy getting everything set up before the storm hit. The tent only took a few minutes to erect. All his supplies and saddle were crammed inside, barely leaving room for him to squeeze in. He brought his horses in close and staked them, driving the pens deep into the ground. The lightning and thunder were almost on top of him by then. Knowing he had done all he could to ensure they would be there tomorrow morning, he crawled into his tent to ride out the storm.

When the wind and rain hit, he was crowded in with the flaps tied tight on each end. For a few minutes, he wasn't sure his tent would stand up to it. It sounded almost like a tornado coming through. If it was, he was going to be in some deep trouble. But he couldn't control what would happen, and knowing a tree could come crashing down on his little tent at any moment, he could never relax. He kept a sharp ear tuned toward his horses should they get scared and start acting up. He didn't hear anything from them as the thunder and lightning sounded like a war was taking place outside his little tent. After what seemed like an eternity, the storm gradually passed, and the night became quiet. It was so quiet it was almost scary. He opened the tent flap on the end closest to the horses and saw them standing where he had left them, looking like a couple of drowned rats. With his head sticking out a little farther, he could see a few feet in each direction and saw nothing he needed to do, so he pulled his head back in and prepared for some sleep. After the nerve-racking hour he had just experienced with the storm, he immediately went to sleep.

Amazingly, he slept through the night without waking once. He had convinced himself that no one would be out on a night like this, so he didn't need to worry about unwanted visitors.

It was dark in his tent when he awoke the next morning, so he couldn't tell what time it was. He lay in his bedroll for a long time until he realized he wasn't going back to sleep, so he crawled out and surveyed the damage from the night before. Limbs were blown down everywhere he looked, but he could see no severe damage. He checked his horses and found them to be in fine shape. He rubbed them down and gave them a good talking-to while he worked them over. He saddled the one he intended to ride and strapped the packsaddle on the other one.

All the wood was wet from the storm, so there was no hope of getting a fire going, so he made a meal of peaches and jerky. After eating, he packed his supplies away, mounted up, and headed north. He had no hopes of picking up tracks of the murderers after the storm, so the best he could hope for would be word of mouth at one of the towns up ahead. But he wasn't even sure they came this way, so he was basing everything on hope, hoping they came this way and hoping someone had seen them and hoping they lived to tell him about it.

He followed the most used trails and roads and eventually came to another settlement. It wasn't large enough to be called a town, and there was nothing to indicate that it had a name.

He went through his usual routine of visiting the livery stables, the saloons, grocery store and asking everyone he came in contact with if they had seen the men he was hunting. After thirty minutes, he had learned nothing. No one had seen or heard anything of men fitting their description.

He stopped at a small diner and enjoyed a good meal before he rode out. He was tightening the cinches on his saddle and packs when he heard horses coming down the street. When he saw who it was, his heart skipped a beat, but he continued doing what he was doing.

Five men dressed in dirty, ragged confederate uniforms came toward him, walking their horses and turning their heads from side to side as they rode. The second thing he noticed was that one was riding a black horse with four stockings, and another was riding a gray horse.

He removed the thong from his pistol and loosened the rifle in its boot, and continued to fumble with the cinches. The five men approached him and rode on past while looking him over good. He felt their eyes bore holes through him, but he appeared not to notice them as they continued down the street. Once they had passed and not looking at him, he slipped his rifle from the scabbard, levered a round into the barrel, and laid it across his saddle, pointed at their backs.

They must have heard when he levered the round into the barrel. All of them jerked around facing him, but he had them covered. "Hold it right there, I've got you covered, now drop your guns and get off those horses."

Before Jim realized what was happening, the five split into five directions and opened fire on him as they scattered. They were spurring their horses and firing over their shoulders as they raced away, so none of the bullets came close to Jim, but it was enough to cause him to duck down behind his horse. By the time he realized they were getting away and brought his rifle up to shoot, only one was in sight. He was over a hundred yards away, beating his horse to get as much speed out of him as possible when Jim set his sights on the man and pulled the trigger. He thought for a second he had missed, but then the man slowly slid to the side and crashed to the ground. Jim jacked another round into the chamber and looked for another target, but they were all gone.

The residents and merchants of the little settlement slowly came out to see what the shooting was about. The ones closest to the body in the street cautiously walked up to check his condition, saw he was dead, and looked to see where the shot came from.

There was no doctor or lawman within twenty miles, so when Jim told them who the dead man was, they patted him on the back and thanked him for taking one of them out of their community.

Jim searched the man's pockets and found only the usual matches, tobacco, and small change. Jim asked the people gathered if they would see that he got buried somewhere. He gave them the money from the man's pockets to help with the cost of the burial.

That was the second man he killed. Somehow he couldn't find it in his heart, mind, or soul to feel bad about it. He probably could have gotten more of them if he had more experience at this. He was determined to be better prepared the next time their trails crossed.

He had to pull himself away from the citizens. They wanted to treat him to a meal or anything else they could do to show appreciation for what he had done. They had heard about the robberies and murders those men had committed, and they felt like Jim had saved them from a bad experience.

He finally convinced them to let him get on the trail of the bad guys before they got completely away and did harm to someone else.

He found the tracks of one of the horses where he cut through between two buildings as he raced away. He locked onto that track and followed it out of town, through a grove of trees, and across a small creek. From there, it curved back toward the main trail, still heading north. Following the tracks was easy, for the man kept at a fast lope until he was a mile or so up the trail. The tracks indicated the horse slowed to a trot when another set of tracks joined the first. The other two joined the first two a little further down the road. The tracks indicated they had sat talking for a few minutes before they moved on.

Jim knew he couldn't be more than thirty minutes behind, but he was worried about catching them. They would be expecting someone to follow them.

He sat for a few minutes, thinking about what he should do. If they were waiting for him, they could kill him before he even knew they were there. That thought made him stop and rethink his next move.

What in the world was he doing chasing these men anyway? He was not cut out for this kind of stuff. He was mad, hurt, and sad when he started after them. He knew he should leave it to the professionals. But how many more people would lose their lives before the law caught up to them, if they ever did? The law in Virginia was not going to be looking for them for crimes they committed in Tennessee. The law in Tennessee was not interested in crimes they committed in Virginia or any other state. So, every time they crossed a state line, their slate was wiped clean, as far as the law in that state was concerned. If they were ever going to pay for killing his parents, it was up to him to do it.

With his mind made up about that, he sat thinking about his next step. All he could come up with was to stay on their trail until something happened and then play it by ear. But he was determined to be more prepared the next time they met.

Their tracks indicated they were not in a hurry, so he followed at a leisurely pace. He didn't want to come upon them before he was ready, and he didn't want to lose their trail either. There wasn't a lot he could do except follow the tracks.

He followed along for almost a mile when his horses suddenly threw their heads up and flared their noses like they were going to whiny. He jerked his horse to the left, put the spurs to him, and darted into the brush. When he was far enough off the trail to be out of sight of anyone waiting to ambush him, he pulled his horses to a stop. After listening for a few minutes and not hearing anything, he had no clue who or what had alerted his horses.

He sat with his rifle in his hands, waiting. After a few more minutes, he dismounted and, with his rifle held at the ready, moved back toward the trail. When he had a clear view for fifty yards in each direction, he crouched down behind a bush to wait. Often the first to move is the first to die, so he was determined not to be that person. He waited for what he thought was probably thirty minutes and nothing happened, but he knew his horses well enough to know they wouldn't react the way they did without a good reason. He waited, more determined than ever not to give his position away.

He was concentrating on the trail before him when he suddenly thought they could be slipping up behind him. The feeling was so strong that he whirled around, ready to fire. Two men were just stepping out of the brush near his horses. They were concentrating on his horses and had not seen him yet, so he had the advantage for now. He recognized them by their dirty confederate uniforms. Before they spotted him, he carefully aimed at the one closest to him and pulled the trigger. Before that one hit the ground, he levered another round in the chamber and fired another shot. The second man spun around with a bullet in his chest and collapsed to the ground. The first one was on his knees, holding his chest and watching the blood flow between his fingers. He looked up at Jim with a shocked look and said, "You killed me."

"Yeah, I did, just like you killed my mom and pop, you sorry piece of trash."

The man was still holding his pistol but didn't look like he had the strength or desire to use it, but Jim wasn't taking any chances. He was ready if the man tried to use it. The waiting didn't take long. The man slowly leaned forward, fell on his face, twitched a couple of times, and didn't move again.

CHAPTER 4

Jim turned back to the trail expecting to see their two friends coming to help them, but the trail was empty. He crouched down behind the bush again and waited to see what the two remaining crooks would do.

After a fifteen-minute wait and nothing happened, he assumed the other two had ridden on ahead, expecting these two to handle the job and catch up.

When it became apparent they were not going to come to check on their friends, Jim returned to the bodies and went through their pockets. As usual, there wasn't much that he could use, but he took what they had and put it in his pocket. They were so dirty he felt like he needed to wash his hands afterward. Their guns were not any better than his, but they may come in handy before this search was over, so he gathered them up and put the handguns in his saddle bags and tied the rifles to the pack saddle on the pack horse. He then slowly moved through the brush and trees toward where he thought they were waiting for him. After a thirty-minute stalk, he found two horses tethered to trees. Tracks leading away indicated the other two had ridden on. He followed the tracks on foot far enough to be convinced they weren't waiting to ambush him.

He returned to the horses, removed the saddles, and turned them loose to find their way.

When he took to the trail again, he was more aware of his horses' reactions than ever before. They had saved his neck today, but he may not be so lucky the next time.

He followed the tracks until it was time to make camp. He planned to stay on their trail until they stopped somewhere, and he could get the drop on them if possible. His nerves were stretched as tight as a bowstring, knowing they could get the drop on him at any time. His back and neck were hurting from the strain, but he knew of nothing he could do about it except try to relax tonight and get some sleep.

He found a thick stretch of woods with lots of underbrush, rode his horses through the brush until he came to a small open place, and decided to make this his home for the night.

With a small fire going, just large enough to heat his coffee water, he made do with the few supplies he had. It wasn't much, but he figured it might be a lot more than he would have some night before this chase was over.

He was hunched over his small fire, eating from a can of beans, when his horses threw their heads up and looked toward the trail. Before they could make a sound, he was into the brush with the hammer reared back on his revolver. He had a good view of his camp, but the darkness had closed in, so he couldn't see much farther than the faint light his campfire was putting out. He waited to see what had alerted his horses and was about to think it was a false alarm when one of them whinnied and got an answer from the direction of the trail.

He only had his handgun with him, hoping this didn't turn into a gun battle. He was definitely at a disadvantage if it came to that.

After another minute, he heard horses coming up the road. He was well hidden with his revolver ready when the murderer's two horses he had turned loose earlier, walked into the firelight.

Jim was so tense that he almost fell over when he saw them. He waited, thinking this could be a trap, but after another five minutes and nothing happened, he decided the horses had followed his looking for companionship.

He returned to his fire, finished his meal, and turned in for the night. He looked at the sky and saw no indication of another storm like last night, and somewhere along the way, he fell asleep and dreamed of Jenny, but when he awoke before daylight, he couldn't remember his dreams. It took a few seconds to get his thoughts together and realize where he was. When it all came back to him, he asked himself again what he was doing here. But he was still determined to see this thing through to the end.

He got himself together and heated the leftover coffee from the night before. A cold biscuit leftover from some previous meal, a stick of jerky, and coffee made up his breakfast. He went through the motions of saddling his horse and packing his few supplies. When everything was ready, he rode to the trail and found the tracks of the two remaining outlaws.

He was in no hurry to catch them on the trail. He hoped to come upon them in a town and get the local law to help him take them into custody. But when he came to the next town, he found there was no law. No sheriff, no town marshal, no law of any kind. When he asked at the cafe where he was having lunch, he was told the town Marshall was killed the day before by a couple of men who rode in and robbed the general store and killed the owner. The Marshall confronted them as they left the store, and they shot him down with no more thought than if he was a rabid skunk.

The waitress was in her late forties, maybe older, it was hard to tell the way she was dressed. She was a little on the plump side with sprinkles of gray in her brown hair. She looked like she had worked hard all her life, and it was showing.

"Did you see the men who did it?"

"Oh, yes," the waitress said, "they came here and ate, walked across the street, robbed the store, and killed the Marshall like it was just another day's work for them."

"What did they look like?"

"They were the dirtiest men I think I ever saw. You could smell them from across the room. I don't know how they could stand to be around each other."

"Can you tell me how they were dressed?"

"They were wearing what had once been confederate uniforms. But I would be ashamed to be associated with anyone who was that dirty."

Jim continued asking questions as long as the lady was willing to talk, "Did you see which way they went when they rode out of town? I'm assuming they left town."

"Oh, they rode in from the south and out to the north. What is your interest in them?"

"There were five of them when they attacked my home, killed my mom and pop, and burned all the buildings. I've been on their trail now for over a week. It looks like I'm still about a day behind, but I'll catch them if someone else doesn't beat me to it."

"Well, I hope you catch them, but watch yourself. Those men will gun you down without blinking an eye."

"I know, they've tried a couple of times already, but I've been pretty lucky so far."

Jim finished his meal and walked out to the boardwalk in front. He stood for a few minutes, stretching his back and letting his legs get used to holding his weight again after being in the saddle for so long.

He was looking up and down the street, dreading getting back in the saddle, when he noticed a paper hanging from a beam supporting the porch roof. Out of curiosity, he walked over to see what it said. What he saw caused him to do a double take, and then he looked both ways up and down the street again, snatched the paper down, folded it, and put it in his pocket. He quickly tightened the cinch on his saddle, mounted, and rode out of town at a gallop. When he was away from town, and no one was around, he stopped to reread the paper.

He got a sick feeling in his stomach and thought he would throw up. There was a very good likeness and a full description, including his full head of reddish-blond hair. The heading across the top of the page read:

WANTED

FOR MURDER

$500.00 REWARD

JIM CARTER

5'8", 180 LBS

REDDISH-BLOND HAIR

BLUE EYES

Contact the sheriff of Surgoinsville, Tennessee

He couldn't help but wonder how they knew so much about him. Jim folded the wanted notice and stuck it in his shirt pocket. "Well, if I survive this, that'll be something to show my grandkids."

From here on, he would have to be doubly cautious because every lawman and bounty hunter in the country would be looking for him. Five hundred dollars was a lot of money for the everyday working man. Most men didn't make over a dollar a day if they were punching cows or working in a store or factory.

While he was pondering on this, he was riding north on the road to where ever. This area was new to him, so all he could do was follow the road, knowing it would bring him to a town sooner or later. He couldn't ride in when he got there and start asking questions. He would have to wait until after dark when the chances of being recognized were much smaller. If he had some way to change his appearance, that would be a big help, but with no way to do that, he would have to make do with what he had.

It was late in the day when he began to see signs of more traffic on the road, which made him believe he was nearing a settlement of some size.

His suspicions were confirmed when he topped the next hill and saw the little town spread out before him. Lights were just beginning to show in the windows of the houses and businesses.

He rode his horse off the trail and dismounted in a thick grove of trees on the hill overlooking the town. He loosened the cinch on the saddle to give his horse a little extra breathing room and settled down to wait until the time was right to enter the town.

He was so exhausted that he only wanted to rest a few minutes before even thinking about what he would do next. He retrieved a strip of jerky from his pack, took his canteen, and found a spot where he could look down on the little town without being seen from below. He leaned back against a large pine tree, chewed on his jerky, and sipped water while thinking about his situation.

On the one hand, he was chasing two men who killed his folks and burned his home, while on the other hand, he was sought by the law for a killing that he knew nothing about. He had to avoid being seen by the law and the men he was following. He felt like he was squeezed between a rock and a hard place with no way out. The more he dwelled on it, the more he thought about giving up and doing what Clay Wade and his brother Ed did, sell the livestock and use the proceeds to marry Jenny, if she would have him, and move to Texas and start over. After all, nothing was left for him here but the land, cattle, and horses. He could sell off enough cattle to get the money to rebuild the house and barns, but he didn't know if he wanted to stay in Tennessee or join the rest of his family in Texas. The more he thought about it, the more confused he became. Since there was no family here, if Jenny would agree to marry him and move to Texas, that's what he preferred to do.

Somewhere along there, he fell asleep and dreamed of Jenny. She was in the pool, and he was sitting on the bank watching her frolic in the water, wishing he was in there with her and wondering why he wasn't. He jumped up and started undressing, but just before he removed his trousers, he jerked and was awake, trying to cover his nakedness, when he realized he was still fully dressed. There was no pool and no Jenny. He was disappointed, relieved, and embarrassed at the same time.

He took a few seconds to realize where and why he was there. It was dark, with no moon or stars shining yet, so the only thing he could make out were the lights of the town at the bottom of the hill.

He felt slightly refreshed after the brief nap, but he still felt like, if given a chance, he could sleep for a week. His muscles felt heavy, his eyes felt like they were full of sand, and he itched all over for need of a bath. He promised himself the next water hole he came to would inherit all his body's sweat and dirt.

He took another piece of jerky from his pack and stuck it in his mouth as he walked down the hill toward the town. He didn't know what he would do when he got there, but he would play it by ear and see what happened.

He had his rifle and handgun loaded to the max in case he needed them, but he hoped he only needed them for the two murderers. He didn't want to get into a gunfight with the law, but he would not be strung up without a fight for something he didn't do.

It was only about five hundred yards from where he left his horses to the edge of town, so he made it in about ten minutes and stopped to catch his breath and look the town over before he went any farther.

There was a little foot traffic on the street, but most of the noise came from two saloons farther up the street. That's where he expected to find his prey if they were here.

He was standing behind the corner of the first building he came to, thinking it was probably a shoe repair shop, saddle shop, or something of that nature, because of the smell of leather he was picking up on the slight breeze. The building was dark, so he moved past it to the next one, which was also dark, so he kept on until he came to a building with light inside. He slowly eased his head around the corner and peeked into the window. What he saw made his stomach growl, and he realized how hungry he was. The smell of freshly baked bread hit his nostrils, and he was tempted to go in and have a good meal, but he had to check out the rest of them town first.

There was only one couple in the cafe, and they didn't look like they would cause trouble for anyone, but there was always the danger of some-one else walking in on him.

The town was dark, except for the light from windows shining on the walk and street. That wasn't enough light for anyone to recognize him, so he casually walked down the street and looked in the windows, hoping to see his two men, but he made it to the last building with lights without finding them. He crossed the street and headed back the other way until he came to the first saloon. It was lit up brighter than any of the other buildings. He stopped at the corner of the building, eased up to the win-dow, and looked inside. The bar ran from front to back along the left wall with a mirror behind the bar. There were no stools in front of the bar, so the few patrons were standing or sitting at tables drinking beer or whis-key. He looked at the men and suddenly realized he wouldn't know them if he met them face to face. He only knew their horses, so he turned away from the window and looked at the horses standing hitched in front. He walked along the street behind the horses to keep from exposing himself to the light from the windows. Eight or ten horses were tied along the street, and he didn't see the ones he was looking for. He knew the men were still riding the black and the gray because the men he had already killed were all riding sorrels or bays.

He was standing in the middle of the street scratching his head when someone spoke to him from the shadows, "Looking for something, young fellow?"

Startled, Jim jerked around and dropped his hand to his gun but realized that would be stupid since he didn't know if this man was a threat. Also, Jim was standing in the middle of the street in plain sight while the other man was in the dark. He decided to play like the innocent man who had nothing to hide.

"Well, yes, I am. Who are you?" He asked as he walked toward the voice. When he was closer, he saw a rather large man standing in the shadow at the corner of the saloon.

"I'm Sheriff Scott. Who are you looking for?"

"Well, Sheriff, you are the man I'm looking for. Have you seen two men around town riding a black horse with four white stockings and a gray with black mane and tail?"

"Maybe. Why are you looking for them?"

"Oh, nothing much. They just killed my mom and dad and burned our house and barns. There were five of them, to begin with. I've cut them down to two so far. Have you seen them?"

"Do you know their names?"

"No, I don't even know what they look like. I've only seen them from a distance, so I only recognize their horses."

Jim was now standing about six feet from the sheriff but still couldn't tell much about him except that he was big. He had to stand well over six feet and weigh two hundred fifty pounds or more. Jim could see enough to know he didn't want to get in a fight with him, and he didn't want to have to shoot him either. He was already in enough trouble without a county sheriff's killing on his record.

"Sheriff, you still haven't told me if you've seen them or not."

"Yeah, I saw them. They were here earlier today, had lunch at the cafe, robbed the general store, and killed the owner."

"That seems to be their pattern." Jim told him, "they did the same thing at a town farther south yesterday. I'm always about a day behind them."

"What do you plan to do when you catch up to them?"

"I hope to kill them if it's the last thing I ever do."

"I hope you catch them. Are you a lawman?"

"No, I'm just a man looking for the men who killed my folks."

"You won't find them here. They left town as soon as they finished their robbing and killing."

"Which way did they go when they left?"

"The road goes northwest from here. I followed them to the county line. That's as far as my authority goes. That's about ten miles out."

"Thank you, Sheriff; I guess I'll be on my way then."

"You be careful, young man. By the way, what's your name?"

Jim almost let his name slip out before he thought about the wanted poster. The only name that came to mind instantly was "Clay Wade."

CHAPTER 5

"Well, Clay Wade, keep your eyes open and your gun handy because if you catch up to them, you're gonna need both of them."

"Thanks, Sheriff." Jim turned and walked as casually as he could toward the end of town when the sheriff called out, "Hey, Jim." Jim stopped with his heart in his throat,

He turned, half-facing the sheriff with his rifle casually pointed in the sheriff's direction, expecting to see a gun pointed at him, "The name is Clay, Clay Wade."

"Sure, well, you be careful, Clay Wade."

Jim was afraid to turn his back on the sheriff, but he had no other choice, so he turned and casually walked out of town. He kicked it in high gear and sprinted up the hill to his horses. He needed to get away from here as soon as possible. He could just see the sheriff getting a posse together to come after him.

He was completely out of breath when he reached the top of the hill and rushed to where he had left his horses. They weren't where they were supposed to be. He was shocked. Did they get loose and wander off, or did someone stumble upon them and take them?

It was too dark to make out any tracks, so he searched the immediate area hoping they had worked loose and wandered off, but the longer he looked, the more certain he was that someone had taken them.

He was mad enough to chew nails, but he could do nothing until daylight tomorrow.

He had no bedroll, nothing to eat or drink, and everything he owned was on his horses. He had enough money to buy another horse and supplies, but that would mean going into town where someone could recognize him.

He stomped around in the trees and brush, looking for some clue, but in the dark, that was hopeless. He finally accepted that he was stuck here for the night and settled down on a patch of leaves to get some sleep.

He tossed and turned all during the night and was glad when there was enough light to see tracks.

While stomping around in the dark last night, he messed up most of the signs, so he walked a circle looking for tacks where they left the area. When he found them, there were tracks of three horses. He could tell by the way the tracks lined up that the rider of the third horse was leading his two. The tracks were fresh enough that he had no trouble following them. He started following at a trot but soon realized this was likely to be a long process, and he couldn't afford to get tired out before he found them. He settled into an easy walk that he planned to stick to until he found his horses and the thief who had taken them.

He hoped the thief was someone local who wouldn't go far because he wasn't accustomed to this walking. High-heeled riding boots were fine for riding, but they were murder on your feet if you had to walk very far.

The tracks led him around the town's south side, then circled back to the east after getting past the town. That made him think the thief was someone local who knew where he was going and didn't want anyone to see him with two extra horses.

He followed the tracks over and around hills, across creeks, up more hills, and finally came out on a well-worn trail. The tracks were as plain as day, so he quickly picked up the pace, thinking he was getting close. The trail wound around the hills and valleys, across more creeks, and finally, about mid-afternoon, when he felt his feet and legs couldn't take any more, he reached the top of a low hill, looked down on a log cabin with a corral in back, a small shed, and five horses in the corral. He felt great relief when he saw two of them were his. He quickly moved into the brush beside the trail and crouched behind a bush. A trickle of smoke drifted from the pipe on the roof, apparently from the kitchen stove, but other than that, there was no sign of life.

He was so tired from the long walk that he was glad to sit back and wait for them to make the first move. He had to know how many people he was dealing with and come up with some idea of how he would get his horses back without getting shot. A horse thief probably wouldn't hesitate to shoot another horse thief any more than he would hesitate to shoot this horse thief if he had to.

He had a good view from the top of the low hill about a hundred yards from the front of the cabin. The five horses were content to stand and swat flies, so there was no movement in their vicinity, or they would be watching it instead of sleeping on their feet.

He found a good size tree to lean back against, removed his boots to let his feet air out, and relaxed after the long walk. He laid his head back against the tree, and before he knew it, he was dozing, half asleep. It was impossible to keep his eyes open sitting there. He tried thinking of something to keep him awake, but his eyes kept closing.

The sun was almost down, and the air was cooler when he came fully awake, stretched his muscles, and tried to wake up. He was still so tired and sore that he was having trouble doing it until he saw movement be-hind the cabin. His eyes popped open, and he sat up and reached for his rifle. A man was walking from the house to the outhouse and didn't seem concerned about anyone seeing him. He wasn't wearing a gun or carrying a rifle, so he didn't feel like he was in danger. After a reasonable time, the man left the outhouse, went to the shed, brought out a bucket of feed for the horses, gave each a scoop, threw the bucket back toward the shed, and returned to the house.

Just before it was completely dark, a light showed in the front win-dow, and more smoke came from the stove pipe. Someone was preparing their supper. That thought made his stomach growl and reminded him that he hadn't eaten in over twenty-four hours. He thought, "if I play my cards right, that may be my supper, so you fix a good one, Buddy."

When it was about as dark as it would get, he checked his guns and moved down the hill to the side of the house. He stood by the wall for a minute, and when he didn't hear any noise from inside, he was pretty sure there was only one man. He eased up to the first window and looked inside. From what he could see, only one room served as the kitchen, liv-ing, dining, and bedroom. One lamp sat on the kitchen table, and one man sat at the table, eating and drinking what was probably coffee.

Jim watched him for a few minutes, and when he showed no sign that anyone was in the room with him, Jim moved to the next window, which was on the other side of the front door. From that window, he could see more of the room. Along the wall opposite the kitchen were four bunk beds lined up end to end. That end of the room was pretty dark, but Jim thought he could make out bodies in two of the beds. There was another window in the kitchen wall, around the corner from where he was, so he quietly moved around the corner to that window where he had a better view of the entire room. The man at the table had his back to Jim, and the two in the bunks were across the room directly in front of him.

As his eyes adjusted to the dim light, he made out more objects he hadn't seen before. The one that caught his interest first was the jug sitting by the bunk where one of the men was sleeping. Jim guessed that man was probably drunk out of his mind, but he wouldn't bet his life on it.

The man at the table was eating and drinking, and the third man in the bunk rolled over, grunted, pulled the blanket up to his chin, and started snoring again.

That accounted for all the men. There were three horses, plus his two, in the corral, so he was satisfied.

A door in the kitchen's back wall was right behind the man eating at the table. Jim quietly moved to that door, tested the latch, and found that it moved easily. He drew his handgun, shoved the door open, and stepped in right behind the man at the table. Before he could move, Jim placed the barrel of his gun on the back of his head and said, "Howdy, horse thief, I'm here to take my horses back. Do you have any objection?" He watched the two on the bunks, but they must be drunk or dead tired, for they never moved.

Jim made sure the man wasn't wearing a gun, quietly moved around the room, collected all the guns he could find, and placed them outside the back door. The two in the bunks never moved except to snore.

When he was sure there were no more guns in the house, he returned to the table and started eating. The cook had fixed enough for three, so there was plenty left. Jim sat at the table where he could keep an eye on all three while he ate. No one said anything, but he could tell the man at the table with him was nervous and plotting something. Jim's gun was lying on the table by his right hand. The man was on his left, so he would have to go through Jim to get to it. When Jim thought the man was about to make some move, maybe cause a racket to wake up the other two, he picked up his gun and cocked it, "Don't even think about it, friend. You stole my horses. That makes you a horse thief, so I won't hesitate to shoot you dead and your two friends over there. So whatever you're thinking, forget it unless you're ready to die."

He continued to eat until he was full, poured a cup of coffee, picked up his pistol, and motioned for the man to get on his feet. With his gun in one hand and coffee in the other, he prodded the man out the back door and told him to go to the barn and get his horses ready to travel.

All this time, the man had not said one word. Jim didn't even know if he could talk, but that was okay. He didn't want to hear anything from him anyway.

Jim watched every move he made while standing where he could see the cabin. He ensured his horses were properly saddled and the pack saddle was loaded and secure. When the man finished, Jim told him to lead his horses out of the corral. Jim turned, putting his horse between him and the thief, and stepped into the saddle. "Now open that gate and drive those horses out."

"Now, wait a minute, you can't do that. That'll leave us with no way to go anywhere."

"Well, isn't that just too bad? That didn't bother you when you took my horses and left me with no way to go anywhere, did it? Open the gate, or I can shoot them. That will serve the same purpose. The choice is yours, but do it now or get out of the way."

"Okay, okay, don't shoot."

The gate was thrown open, the horses driven out, and Jim fell in behind and drove them out of the valley on the way he came in. They kept to the road, and Jim followed along. He was pretty sure this road would take him back to the town with the big sheriff, but he didn't plan to stop in to say hello. But he wanted to follow the trail on the other side of town, so he would skirt it to the north and continue northwest. That's the direction the sheriff told him the murderers went.

It must have been close to dawn when he saw a few lights ahead. The three horses were still ahead and would continue into town, so he cut off the trail to the right. It was too dark to see if there was a trail, so he let his horse have his head and pick his way through the jumble of brush, trees, and rocks.

The sun came up bright and revealed the heavily forested mountains surrounding him. His horse was having difficulty finding a way through and around the mess.

After an hour or more, he finally came out on the road northwest of the town. He couldn't make out any useful tracks since it had been two days since the killers passed this way, but he trusted the sheriff had told him the truth since he would have no reason to lie to him.

He was so tired he could hardly keep his eyes open and sit in the saddle, so he started looking for a good place to stop for some rest. He found it a few minutes later when he came to a small creek that crossed the road and continued down the hill to his left. He turned right up the stream, staying in the water simply because that was the easiest path for his horses. After a hundred yards, he came to a flat area on the side of the creek, rode out of the water, and dismounted. His knees buckled under his weight, but he held onto the horn of his saddle until he was steady on his feet. He unbuckled the cinch on his saddle, let it fall to the ground, and did the same for the pack saddle. After fishing the stakes from the pack, he drove them deep into the ground and ensured his horses were secure, and then he crashed with his head on his saddle and was sleeping almost immediately.

He roused up a few times just long enough to see his horses were still there and content and fell asleep again.

Several hours later, around mid-afternoon, he was fully awake and felt like a new man. He dug some jerky from his pack to chew on while he saddled his horse and secured the packs on the other. There were still several hours of daylight left, and he intended to make the most of it.

He followed the creek down to the road and checked both ways as he approached. When he didn't see or hear anyone, he rode onto the road and checked for fresh tracks, as had become his habit. Finding nothing of interest, he put his horse in a fast trot and, after a mile or so, increased it to a slow gallop for almost an hour.

He alternated between a trot and a gallop for the rest of the day until the horses began to tire, and then he let them walk until it must have been almost midnight. He slept for the rest of the night on the side of the hill overlooking the road.

Nothing disturbed them during the night, and he was up early and on the trail before sunrise.

He pushed his horses hard all day, trying to make up for the day he lost.

Toward evening, he came to a farmhouse sitting off the road to his right and stopped to watch for a few minutes. A man came from the barn carrying a bucket with milk sloshing over the rim and going toward the house. He didn't see anyone else around and decided to take this opportunity to ask about the men he was after.

He rode to within twenty feet of the front door and called, "Hello, the house!"

The same man opened the door only a moment later, but he had exchanged the bucket of milk for a long-barreled shotgun. It only took one glance to know this man knew how to use it, so Jim sat with both hands in plain sight, and when the man stepped out onto the porch, Jim removed his hat and said, "Excuse me for interrupting your day, but I was passing by and wondered if you have seen a couple of men I've been looking for.

Two of the dirtiest men you have ever seen wearing old confederate uniforms. One of them rides a black, the other a gray. Have you seen anyone fitting that description?"

"Why do you want to find those sorry scoundrels?"

"I take it from that that you have seen them. You're still alive, so you are doing better than others who've seen them."

"I have my boy to thank for that." The man had lowered the shotgun but watched Jim very carefully.

Jim asked him, "How did that happen?"

The man pointed toward the barn, "He was up in the hay loft throwing down hay for the cows and horses when he saw them coming up the road. We always keep an old scattergun in the barn, so he picked it up and waited to see what they wanted. They rode up to about where you are, just sat their horses looking around, and didn't say anything. Finally, one started to get off his horse, and the other drew his gun when the boy told them to stay where they were and state their business. I heard the noise and looked out the window there." He pointed to the window beside the front door. "They didn't know where the boy was, so they were caught with their pants down, so to speak."

"They were nervous as a cat in a room full of rocking chairs. They didn't know which way to turn. Finally, one said they only wanted to water their horses; there was no need to get all riled up. But they looked like the scum of the earth, so we weren't taking any chances. I opened the front door holding my shotgun and stepped out. They were covered from two sides and didn't know where the other gun was. You should have seen them squirm. So I told them there was a creek about a half mile up the road. Help yourself to all the water you want. They didn't like that one bit, and you could see in their faces that they had come here with other intentions."

"I'm sure you're right about that. I've followed them for almost a week. They've killed four men and a woman that I know of and robbed several stores. You were fortunate your son saw them coming."

"We stood guard the rest of the day, but you're the first person we've seen since they left."

"When did this happen?" Jim asked.

"That was early this morning; I had just finished milking old Dolly when they showed up. It added some excitement to a usually dull day."

"I'm assuming they went northwest when they left here?"

"They went out to the road and turned right, so if they stuck to it, they would go northwest."

"How far is it to the next town?" Jim asked.

"It's only about three miles, as the crow flies."

Jim replaced his hat, thanked the man for the information, turned his horse, rode back to the road, and turned northwest.

Jim thought as he rode, "*That was this morning, probably around six or seven. These people begin their days early. I'm still about eight or ten hours behind if my timing is right.*"

He picked up the pace and hoped to make it to the town before nightfall to look it over while he could still see. But a few minutes later, he came to the creek the man mentioned, and the water looked so inviting he just had to stop and get cleaned up. It had been too long, and he knew he looked and smelled awful. He tied his horses and stripped to the skin and eased into the water. It felt so good that he just sat and soaked until his skin wrinkled. He washed his hair and got his shaving gear, and shaved. He felt so much better that he promised himself he wouldn't go that long without bathing again. He used his dirty clothes to dry himself and got into clean clothes. He noticed he had one clean shirt left. He would have to do something about that when he reached the next town.

Twenty minutes later, he was sitting at the edge of the little town, looking up the main street. The sign said this was Hazard. He hoped that was the name of the town and not a prediction of what was to come. When he reached the first house, the lights began showing in the windows. He sat on his horse, watching the activity on the street and looking for the two horses he would recognize.

A couple of riders came and went, but none came his way, so he stayed where he was until it was completely dark and felt safe to ride into town.

He rode slow, not wanting to attract attention, until he saw a white or gray horse standing at a hitch rack in front of a saloon. He spotted the gray horse first because he stood out in the dark better than the black one next to him.

His heart skipped a couple of beats, and he could hardly control himself. He was shaking so bad he knew he couldn't face them like this. He rode past the two horses and tied up in front of the building next door. The saloon was one of the few businesses open, so he pulled his rifle from the boot and jacked a round into the chamber. He then checked his revolver and returned it to the holster when he was satisfied everything was working as it should.

With the rifle in his right hand hanging by his right side, he approached the first window of the saloon. It was so dirty with dust, spider webs, and flies that he could hardly see in, but he made out several men sitting at a table drinking and a couple of others standing at the bar. None of them were the two he was after. He took a step back, looked at the front of the building, and noticed a second floor above the bar. Another look in the window, and he spotted stairs at the end of the bar leading to the second floor. That must be where his men were, probably entertained up there by a couple of ladies of the night, soiled doves, prostitutes, whatever you want to call them. So, what was he supposed to do now? He could wait out here for them to come out, or he could go in after them. But he didn't know where they were, so waiting for them to come out seemed the best option. But that could take all night, and he didn't want to wait around that long.

CHAPTER 6

He figured when they came down from their frolic upstairs, they would want another drink, so with some time to spare, he looked around town to see what there was for him to do while he waited. A building farther up the street had a light showing in the window, so he walked up there to see what it was. On the way, he checked each building as he passed. He was mainly looking for a sheriff's office or city Marshall, so he would know if he needed to stay out of sight. When he saw no sign of an officer of the law, he felt a little better about his situation. Maybe that's why the two murderers were still hanging around. There was no law in this little town.

He looked in the lighted window and saw only one older couple eating at a table. He removed his hat and pushed through the screen door. The place was spotless, with white tablecloths and napkins at each table, the floor looked like it had just been scrubbed, and the smell of food had his stomach growling before he sat down.

The man and woman looked his way when he entered. He nodded and tried to look innocent and not attract attention.

He took a seat in the back where he could watch the door. After he was seated, he noticed another door in the back corner, leading out back, probably to the privy, for the use of their customers.

It seemed like there was a pretty girl everywhere he stopped to eat, and this was no exception. She was about five foot three, with blue eyes, black hair hanging halfway down her back, and lips made for kissing. When she first appeared at his elbow to take his order, he looked up into those blue eyes, saw those lips, and was speechless. He stammered and stuttered and couldn't get one word out. Finally, she asked him, "Would you like to start with coffee while I get your supper?"

The voice was enough to make any man leave home. It was so soft and sweet that he couldn't think of anything to say. He just nodded as he stared at her. She smiled and showed the most beautiful teeth he had ever seen. He couldn't take his eyes off her as she walked away. She was probably seventeen, maybe eighteen, and had a body with everything in the right place. He was in a trance until she came back with his coffee. She placed the cup on the table and poured his coffee. He was looking into her eyes while she poured the coffee and couldn't take them off her. She looked at him and smiled; a look came over her face, making his heart flutter.

He was in love. He thought he was in love with Jenny, but now he knew he wasn't after seeing this girl. They stared at each other for almost a full minute. There was a mutual attraction that neither could deny. She put her hand on his shoulder and said, "We close in one hour."

"I'll be here to walk you home."

"Okay."

They continued to look into each other's eyes until the spell was broken when one of the other patrons called her name and asked for more coffee.

Victoria: The most beautiful name he had ever heard. He would call her "Vicki"; he said it aloud and loved how it rolled off his tongue.

He was in a daze when his food came, and he noticed his coffee was cold and had not taken a sip.

"You haven't touched your coffee. Is something wrong?" There was that voice again. He couldn't get past how soft and sweet it was.

"No, everything is perfect; you are so beautiful I can't take my eyes off you."

"That's sweet, but I'm afraid you will have to because I have to get back in the kitchen."

"Oh, I need more coffee if it isn't too much trouble. This one has gotten cold."

"You did that deliberately, didn't you?" She asked with a beautiful smile.

He smiled, "No, but you've given me an idea."

She slapped him lightly on the shoulder and went to the kitchen.

He watched her walk away and thought how glad he was that he had gotten a bath and shaved.

He dug into the food like he hadn't eaten in months. The coffee was the best he had had since the last cup his mom had made for him. That thought brought him back to reality and made him realize where he was and the danger he could be in if a lawman or bounty hunter should recognize him.

He was watching the clock to see how much longer before she closed the café, and he would walk her home. He hoped she lived a long way out in the country.

He ate slowly, enjoying the food and trying to make it last until she got off work.

He had just finished his food and was on his third cup of coffee when two dirty men wearing old confederate uniforms came in the door. They were more than half drunk, loud, and obnoxious as they staggered to a table, slammed their fist on it, and demanded service. They looked around at the other diners, "What are you staring at? Ain't you ever seen a real man before?"

Jim recognized trouble as soon as he saw them. He slipped the revolver from his holster and held it under the table. He has been looking for these men but didn't want to find them where innocent people could get hurt. He kept his head down and pretended to ignore them. One of them stared at him, but when he saw Jim was ignoring him, he sat down, pounded the table again, and shouted, "How about some service here!"

The older couple got up and hurriedly left the diner.

Victoria came from the kitchen carrying a coffee pot and two cups. She looked nervous but smiled and said, "Hello, men, what'll it be, coffee for starters?"

"Well, lookie here, how about some of you for starters?" He put his arm around her waist and pulled her tight against him. She pushed away and said, "I am not on the menu, so keep your hands off. We only serve food here."

"Well, we can change that, honey. Come back here." He grabbed her and pulled her down on his lap. She slapped him across the face and tried to pull away, but she couldn't break the hold. She hit him again, and he laughed harder and said, "I like 'em with some fight in 'em. We gonna have a good time."

Jim rose from his table, walked up behind them, and laid the pistol barrel across the man's head above his ear. He crumbled to the floor as Jim took hold of Victoria and lifted her to her feet.

The second outlaw watched the show and laughed until he saw Jim hit his partner. He came off his chair and went for his gun. Jim pointed his gun at him and said, "If you want to die, just pull that gun."

The man dropped the gun back in the holster and raised his hands. Jim told him, "Take your filthy partner, get out of here, and don't come back."

The man seemed to have sobered up in a hurry. He looked Jim up and down and, without a word, picked up his partner and half carried half dragged him out the door. Jim followed them and watched to make sure they kept going. They dragged and staggered down the street toward the saloon.

Jim went back inside and found Victoria, "Are you okay?"

She leaned against him, "Thank you so much. I was scared to death. I don't know what would have happened if you weren't here."

"They won't get a chance to do anything else. How long before you close?"

"We're closing now." She went to the front door, locked it, and turned down the lamp in the dining room. "I'll clean up tomorrow morning. Let's get out of here."

Her mother was working in the kitchen and agreed it was time to leave.

The three of them went out the back door and locked it. "Mom, this is; I don't know your name."

"I'm Jim Carter, ma'am."

"Jim Carter, Jim, this is my mom, Teresa Simpson."

"Ms. Simpson, I'm pleased to meet you and your beautiful daughter. It's easy to see where she gets her beauty."

"Well, aren't you the silver-tongued devil, but you keep it up, and I'll steal you from my daughter."

The walk to their house was a short two blocks, but they were glad Jim was with them. He was invited in for coffee but refused, telling them he had a job to do.

Mrs. Simpson bid him a good night and went inside.

Victoria asked, "Does it have anything to do with those men?"

Not wanting to worry her, he said it didn't, but he didn't think she believed him.

"I'll see you at breakfast." He told her.

"You better. I'm gonna hold you to it."

She surprised him when she stepped up and planted a long sweet kiss on his lips.

He was so stunned he staggered back and missed the step off the porch. She laughed and waved as he walked backward down the walk, still smiling.

He was still in a daze when he reached the saloon where he expected to find the two killers. He looked in the window but didn't see them inside, so he pushed through the bat wing doors and walked to the bar. The bartender approached him and asked what he was having.

"Where are those dirty confederate slobs who were here earlier?"

"They returned a short while ago, and one had a bad knot on his head. They were talking about killing some cowboy. Would that be you?"

"Probably, they were causing trouble for the waitress down at the café."

"You better be careful, those guys look like trouble, and I mean real trouble. They left here looking for you."

"Good," Jim said, "Because I'm looking for them too. Did you see which way they went when they left?"

"All I saw was they took a left when they went out the door."

"Thanks," he turned to leave, then stopped and turned back and said, "If they come back, tell them to wait for me, I'll be back."

The bartender laughed, "OK, I'll tell them, but you're biting off a mighty big mouth full there."

"I think I can chew it."

"I hope you're right."

Jim left the saloon and turned left down the sidewalk. The night was dark with no moon out yet. The few stars showing weren't doing much good, so the light coming from the windows of houses and businesses that were still open, hoping to catch another sale, was the only light.

With the pistol in his hand, he walked as close to the buildings as he could. At the corner of each building, he stopped to listen and poked his head around the corner to check the alley before continuing.

He was slowly making his way back toward Victoria's house. He had no way of knowing if the men knew where she lived, but that seemed like the most logical place to look, and if she was in danger, that's where he needed to be.

He picked up the pace and was running when he saw her house.

A muffled scream came from the back of the house. He sprinted around the corner and saw two horses galloping away with someone lying across the saddle in front of one of the men. It was too dark to be sure, but he raised his gun for a shot and realized he couldn't shoot. If they had Victoria, he might hit her. He ran to the house's back door and found it standing open and Victoria's mother lying on the floor with blood on her head. He ran to her and saw she was still alive but groggy. She looked up at him but didn't recognize him and just stared. He shook her and asked, "Did those men take Victoria?"

She still did not comprehend what he was saying, so he ran to the kitchen, found a cloth, and wet it from the bucket on the cabinet. When he returned, she seemed a little more aware. He ran the wet cloth over her face and wiped the blood from her forehead. She was coming around and then got a wild, frightened look on her face, tried to sit up, and screamed, "Vicki, where is Vicki, Vicki?"

Jim tried to console her, but she was still groggy and trying to sit up and look for Vicki.

"Ma'am, Ma'am, look at me." He wiped her face again with the wet cloth. That seemed to help her grasp things for a second, but she was still looking for Vicki.

In a relatively calm voice, she looked at Jim and asked, "Did they take Vicki?"

"Yes, Ma'am, I think they did. I got here just a little too late to stop them. I need to get after them if you're going to be okay. Should I get someone to come and stay with you?"

It took a few moments for her to grasp the situation, but finally, she pointed, "Mrs. Damouth, next door."

"Okay, I'll get her here. Let me help you up and get you to a chair."

He put his hands under her arms, lifted her to her feet, and supported her to the closest chair. "I'll be right back."

He sprinted out the door and found the neighbors standing on the porch, trying to see what all the noise was. When he ran around the corner, they darted for their door, but before they could get back inside, he told them what was happening and that the lady next door needed her help. He didn't wait around to see what happened after that. He ran as fast as his legs could carry him to his horses, mounted in less than a minute, and raced out of town after the kidnappers.

A half-moon was peaking over the trees, but it didn't give enough light to find the men's tracks. But he saw them take the road out of town in that direction. He kept his horse in a fast gallop and followed the road for what seemed like a half hour or so before he slowed to think things out a bit. He didn't want to go too far and lose them altogether.

His horses were blowing hard, so he let them walk while he thought about what he could and should do. There wasn't much he could do in the dark, so he stopped and listened, hoping to hear them ahead of him. All was quiet except for the rapid breathing of his two horses. He couldn't hear anything with that noise, so he dismounted and walked up the trail away from them until he could hear clearly. He listened, straining his ears for any sound that would indicate they were nearby. He only heard the wind blowing through the trees overhead and his heart beating fast. He looked around in the dark, hoping to catch a glimpse of a campfire, but then realized they hadn't had time to get a fire going.

When he returned to his horses, they breathed much quieter and slower. He petted them, scratched their ears, and talked to them quietly before stepping into the stirrup and taking his seat in the saddle. He was frustrated, not knowing what to do next. He couldn't go back to town and leave Vicki in the hands of those murderers, and he couldn't continue without possibly losing them in the dark. He decided the best thing he could do was continue on this road and hope for the best. He couldn't bear to think what would happen to Vicki if she was left with those two men overnight.

He was too frightened for Vicki to sit here doing nothing while she was probably being violated, and he was sure they would kill her when they finished with her. He took a chance that they had stayed on the road since it was too dark to see much of anything, and in the trees and underbrush off the road, it would be impossible to see where they were going. Thinking it was a good bet to stick to the road, he continued at a slow gallop, watching and listening for any sign that they were near.

He stopped and listened every few minutes, but he was getting more worried the longer this dragged on. He tried to think how long it had taken him to get his horses and get on the trail. The best guess he could come up with was maybe five minutes, maybe longer, he didn't know, but they were at least that far ahead of him. He only hoped he was still on their trail, that they had not turned off somewhere, and he had missed them.

He kept riding and got more frustrated at the slow pace he had to maintain. He desperately wanted to overtake them before they could harm Vicki, but he didn't want to alert them that he was coming. That would get both of them killed before he could do anything to help her.

He was tired, and his horses were tired, but he couldn't stop.

The thought that he may not even be on their trail was frightening. What if they turned off somewhere? He almost stopped and turned back. Then he wanted to kick himself for not thinking of this earlier. He stopped his horse, dismounted, removed a match from his pocket, and struck it on his pant leg. When the flame flared up, he shielded his eyes for a moment, not wanting to destroy his night vision more than necessary, and brought the match down close to the ground, searching, and hoping for a miracle. After a few minutes and several more matches, he was pretty sure he was still on their trail. The fresh tracks of two horses were there as plain as day. He could only hope they belonged to the men he was after. He breathed a sigh of relief as he got back in the saddle and continued at a faster pace. He felt more comfortable now that he was pretty sure he was on the right track, but he still had to be careful not to ride up on them unexpectedly.

He continued at what he thought was a safe speed but stopped every so often to listen. He was getting more worried as time passed, afraid he would miss them or had already done so. He wanted to go racing ahead as fast as his horses could run. Still, he knew that was a dangerous thing to be thinking, so he did his best to keep his emotions in check and hope for the best

He had been riding all night, and it was close to daybreak when his horses threw up their heads and came to a complete stop. He knew his horses well enough to know that was a danger sign. They would not react that way to another horse or cow, so it had to be a man or a man-made sound that got their attention so quickly.

He listened for a minute or so until he heard a man's voice and then walked his horses back up the trail until he found a suitable place to ride off the trail. After fifty feet, he stopped, threw the reins over a limb, and told his horses to wait.

Pulling his rifle from the sheath, he checked to ensure a round was in the barrel and shoved more cartridges into the magazine until it was full. He then checked his revolver, added a sixth round to the cylinder, and proceeded on foot. He had only gone a hundred feet when he heard sticks breaking. It sounded like someone was getting ready to start a fire, so he took his time, moving as quietly as possible. He wanted to see what was happening before they settled in and started on Vicki.

When he saw movement ahead, he slowly, one step at a time, continued until he had a clear view of their camp. The fire was beginning to flicker but not yet putting out enough light to see anything.

He could only see the people when they moved, so he hadn't located Vicki yet. He moved closer and stopped behind a huge pine tree that must be several hundred years old. The ground was covered in pine needles, allowing him to move without making a sound unless he stepped on a dead limb that had fallen from the tree. Those he could feel with his feet before he put his weight on them.

The sky was getting lighter in the east, and he began gradually making out other details about their camp. A small stream ran by a few feet on the other side of the fire. Their horses were tied near the stream on the other side of the fire from Jim. One of the men removed the saddles and supplies and dropped them near the fire. The second man was still bending over the fire, trying to get it going. He finally spotted what he thought was Vicki lying on her side against a tree a few feet away. She was off to the side and not between him and the fire starter, which was ideal in case a shootout was to take place, and he was pretty sure it would. He was only waiting until both men were close together near the fire so he could cover both simultaneously.

He couldn't tell from here if Vicki was tied, injured, or sleeping. She had been up all night without a stop after working all day at the café, so she had to be dead tired.

He started quietly moving around to where she was lying. He hoped to get her away before the fire got bright enough to show what was happening. Before he had gone more than ten feet, a horse whinnied back up the trail. He knew it had to be one of his who had gotten the scent of the outlaw's horses.

The two men quickly grabbed their guns and took cover, but not before one kicked the fire apart and stepped on the burning branches to extinguish the flame. Jim was cursing his luck but knew there was nothing he could do about it now.

The men were on high alert, which reduced the chances of getting Vicki away, so he crouched down behind a tree trunk and waited to see what would happen.

A scream came from his right where Vicki was lying, and one of the men dashed to shut her up. Before he reached her, Jim rose from his hiding place and, taking quick aim, got off a shot. The bullet spun the man around, and in doing so, the man saw the flash and smoke from Jim's gun and got off a haste shot. It had to be pure luck, but the bullet hit Jim's left arm, causing him to jerk to the left and miss his next shot. The outlaw dived toward Vicki and rolled up behind her. Jim couldn't get another shot at him, so he turned his attention to the other. He was nowhere to be seen, so Jim started backing away into the heavier brush and circling to his right to come up behind Vicki and the man hiding behind her.

The going was extremely slow, trying not to make any noise and favoring the bullet wound in his arm, which was beginning to hurt like the devil. Blood was running down his arm and soaking his shirt sleeve. His hand was bloody and slick, making it hard to hold his rifle, and he found he couldn't lift it to aim anyway, so he laid it aside and pulled his revolver with his right hand. He continued to move toward Vicki, but he was worried about the second man. He didn't know where he was, and that posed a problem.

He kept moving as quietly as possible, but it took a long time to get where he needed to be.

There was movement in the brush, but it was too quiet to tell where it came from. All he could do was keep moving and hope to take the men out before he got too weak or passed out from blood loss. He was already feeling light-headed. He didn't know if that was from loss of blood or the shock of getting shot. He had never been shot before, so he didn't know how he was supposed to feel, but so far, he didn't like the experience. The arm was hurting; he was getting weak and dizzy and didn't know how much longer he could hold on. He had to get this over quickly if he was going to save Vicki.

Frantically, he forced himself forward, pushing the revolver ahead of him. Somewhere along there, he must have passed out. When he came too, he heard the man telling Vicki to stay quiet, or he would put a bullet in her head. From that, he gathered that she must have screamed or made some noise that aroused him from his fainting spell.

He got his bearings straight in his head and pushed forward another few feet. A large tree was right in front of him, so he laid his head on his arm to rest for a moment. He was so weak he could hardly hold his head up but knew he had to keep going, or he would soon be dead, and Vicki would be at the mercy of those two ruthless men. There was no doubt in his mind what that meant for her.

A man was whispering just a few feet from him. It sounded like it was coming from just the other side of the tree right in front of him. He moved slightly to his right to see past the tree and must have made a noise. The man whirled in his direction and fired a shot so quickly that Jim didn't have time to react before the bullet hit him in the shoulder. The hit caused him to flinch and fire his gun, hitting the man in the face. He screamed and fell backward, holding his face in both hands. Blood was running between his fingers and down his arms. The man kept screaming and rolling on the ground for another thirty seconds, then he relaxed and became deathly quiet.

CHAPTER 7

Jim felt the bullet's impact, but it took a moment to realize he was hit again. He felt dizzy, and then the world went black. His vision faded, but he still heard everything around him until that gradually disappeared, and he heard and saw nothing.

Vicki screamed and crawled backward until she bumped into Jim and screamed again. She didn't recognize him with his face buried in the pine straw and blood all over his shoulder, face, and arm. She scrambled away a few feet until she realized he wasn't one of the kidnappers. She looked around to see where the second outlaw was, but not seeing him, she crawled back to Jim and placed her hand on his back. She felt him breathing, so there was hope. He had lost his hat, so she had a partial view of his face. She pulled some pine straw away and recognized the young man who had walked her home last night. "Oh no, Jim," she sobbed. She shook him but got no reaction.

One killer was still out there, and Jim was out of the fight, so she was on her own. When she realized that, she got even more scared. What was she going to do now? Jim's gun lay on the ground beside him. She picked it up, scrambled back into the brush, and hid the best she could while keeping an eye on Jim.

She felt more secure with the gun in her hand, but she was scared out of her wits, and she knew if she got a chance to put a bullet in that man, she wouldn't hesitate to do it. She had hunted and fished with her dad since she was a small girl. He taught her to shoot with a rifle and a pistol, and she had gotten very good with both, so they were no strangers to her.

She pulled the hammer back to full cock, and yelled, "Come and get me, you lousy piece of trash. I have a gun, and I know how to use it. Come on, unless you're afraid to face a girl. I think you're a yellow coward."

She was shaking and crying but determined to do whatever it took. She eased a little farther back into the brush but still could see Jim, and he had not moved. She couldn't tell if he was still alive or not.

A few minutes later, she heard a horse racing away to the northeast. That had to be the second kidnapper giving up. "Just like I thought, you're a yellow coward." She yelled.

She rushed back to Jim to see if there was anything she could do for him.

Having nothing to use for bandages nor medicine to treat a wound, all she could do was try to make him comfortable until she could come up with something.

He was still lying where he fell and looked like he was dead. She gently rolled him onto his back and saw his chest slowly rising and falling, so he was alive, and where there was life, there was hope.

It was full daylight now, and she got a good view of her surroundings. The fire was scattered with only a few smoldering pieces of wood here and there. She gathered them into a pile where the outlaw had started the fire earlier. With a bit of coaxing, she soon had it going again.

The outlaw's horse was tied nearby, so she checked the saddlebags to see if there was anything she could use. A small coffee pot and enough coffee to make a pot or two were all she found that she could use. The man's bedroll smelled so bad she threw it aside and hoped it would keep the varmints away. Then she thought about Jim's horse. It had to be nearby, but she hesitated to leave Jim to look for it.

She added a few more sticks to the fire and checked on him again. He was still out. She couldn't tell if he was sleeping or unconscious. Whatever, it was probably best for him. At least he wasn't hurting.

She got the coffee pot on the fire, and while it was heating, she looked for Jim's horse. It didn't take long to find it, except there were two of them, and one was loaded with supplies. She brought them back to the fire, tied them with the other horse, removed the saddle and packs, and dragged them to the fire.

The body of the dead outlaw was still lying where he fell, and she had to walk past it every time she went to the fire. She knew she had to do something with it, but it was too heavy for her to move. She thought about it for a few minutes and then remembered the rope on Jim's saddle. The outlaw's horse was still saddled, so she brought him up close, looped the rope around the man's ankles, tied the other end to the saddle's horn, and led the horse into the woods. When she was far enough away that she wouldn't have to look at it, she removed the rope from his ankles and left him lying.

When she returned to the fire, she was so tired she couldn't move another step. It was as if someone had pulled a plug and all her energy drained out in a few seconds. She collapsed by the fire and cried.

She was still lying there when she heard the coffee boiling and steam rising from the pot. She rolled over and, using her skirt as a potholder, lifted the coffee pot from the fire and set it on a stone to cool enough to drink.

She checked on Jim and saw he was still out but breathing steadily.

Maybe he was just tired, like she was, and needed sleep, but when she looked at him again, the amount of blood frightened her. She needed to do something, but she didn't know what.

She found another small pot in Jim's supplies, filled it with water from his canteen, and put it on the fire to heat. Rummaging through his pack and saddlebags, she found a clean shirt and decided she could use it for bandages, so when the water had boiled for a couple of minutes, she removed the pot from the fire to let it cool. She then went to Jim and removed enough of his clothes to see the extent of his wounds. The bullets had gone all the way through, one in the upper left arm and the other in the right shoulder just under the collar bone. Neither of them seemed to have hit any vital organs, so if she could stop the bleeding and keep the infection away, she thought he would have a good chance of pulling through. Her knowledge of treating bullet wounds was minimal. The only thing she had to go on was her common sense. It seemed logical to get the bleeding stopped. She soaked a piece of his shirt in hot water and bathed the wounds. When she had removed as much of the blood as she could, she tore the shirt into strips and wrapped them around his arm and shoulder as tight as she could wrap them.

Jim was still resting comfortably or in a coma. Either way, he wasn't feeling the pain.

Before she could convince herself the danger from her kidnappers was over, she walked around the camp area, holding the pistol with her finger on the trigger.

When she returned to Jim, he had not moved but was resting, so taking the bedroll found in his pack, she spread it on the ground beside him and laid down, thinking she would only rest a few minutes.

When she next opened her eyes, it was late afternoon. Jim was still sleeping, which she thought was probably the best thing for him. She didn't know of anything else she could do. Maybe when he awoke, she could fix some broth, or soup, from the supplies she found in his pack.

She checked his bandages and saw only a tiny amount of blood had seeped through.

Not knowing what else to do, she walked around their camp until she came to the horses. They had been standing for over ten hours without water or food and knew they must be hungry and thirsty.

Not familiar with any of the horses, she didn't take any chances of them breaking away from her, so she took them one at a time to drink from the stream, then tied them where they could reach fresh grass. She moved them to a new spot whenever the grass was eaten down.

Jim continued to sleep, but he occasionally tried to move, let out a moan, and grimaced in pain. To Vicki, that was a good sign. She hated to see him lying there and not moving, but she hated to see him in pain. It scared her, thinking he might die and leave her here alone. What would she do then? She couldn't ride off and leave him lying there.

She got the fire going again, made another pot of coffee, and heated a can of beans. Sitting on the bedroll beside him, eating and drinking, she looked into his face and realized he was really handsome. She put her hand on his cheek and felt him stir slightly. After a moment of sitting, looking at his face, on impulse, she leaned over and kissed him. She felt him move, and when she pulled back, his eyes were open and looking at her. She jumped back and covered her mouth, "Jim, you're awake. How do you feel? Are you hungry? You want some coffee?"

He smiled faintly and, in a weak hoarse voice, said, "I could take some more of that."

"Some more of what?" she asked.

"I could take another one, or two, of those kisses if you have any to spare."

She was silent for so long he thought she had taken offense at his suggestion. But then she slowly leaned over him and planted another kiss on his lips. "Will there be anything else for you, sir?"

"What happened to me? Where are the men who kidnapped you?"

"You were shot twice, killed one of them, and the other ran. You've been sleeping since early morning. I was so scared, not knowing if you would ever wake up."

"I think I'm going back to sleep." He whispered, "If you promise to wake me like that again in a few hours." His eyes slowly closed, and he was sleeping again.

She sat looking into his face and smiling, "You sleep as long as you need to. I'll be here when you wake up." And then she remembered she was going to try to feed him something and get him to drink, but it was too late. He needed sleep more than food.

CHAPTER 8

Jim slept through the night, only waking for short periods. Between his naps, she got him to take a few swallows of water and a couple of spoons of broth. She checked his bandages, and later in the day, when he was awake longer than usual, she removed them, cleaned his wounds with warm water, and applied more bandages. He watched her through the entire process and never said a word or showed any signs that he was hurting, but she knew he had to be. There was no sign of infection, for which she was grateful.

When night came, he showed a slight fever and became very restless. She bathed his face and chest with cool water from the stream, which seemed to help. She kept that up for the next two hours until he relaxed and fell into a deep sleep. For the rest of the night, she sat by his side and bathed him with cool water when he got restless. The night was cool, but he kept kicking the blanket off and trying to roll over, but every time he moaned, and his face squinted in pain.

She was pulling the blanket over him when she heard horses on the trail. Her first thought was the other outlaw was coming back, but there was more than one horse, and they were coming from the wrong direction. These sounded like they were coming from the direction of town. Maybe it was someone looking for her. She grabbed the rifle and ran to the edge of the brush, where she could see the trail for a hundred yards or so. When they came around the bend, there were five of them, and a couple looked familiar. When they got closer, she recognized men from her hometown. One of them was Robert Freeman, a young man who had been trying to court her for the last two years. The others were merchants from the town.

The relief was so great she crumpled to the ground and cried. She was still kneeling there when the men rode up to her and dismounted. She got to her feet and rushed to them, threw her arms around Robert, and cried. He held her and stroked her back until she could talk. "Oh, I'm so glad to see you. I didn't know what I was going to do. He's hurt bad and needs a doctor."

"Who's hurt, and what about the kidnappers? What happened to them?"

She was having trouble talking, but she finally got it out. "One is dead, and the other one ran away. But Jim is hurt bad."

"Who is Jim, and what is he doing here?"

"He saw them kidnap me and followed us until they stopped here for the night. Just as they were getting a fire started, Jim came up and shot one of them, and the other ran off, but Jim was shot twice. He needs a doctor bad."

Robert's jealousy was showing through, and he kept asking questions about Jim until one of the older men told him to knock it off, "None of that matters now, let's get the man to the doctor. Where is he hit?"

She told them, "In his left arm and right shoulder."

"Do you think he can ride?"

"I don't think so. He's unconscious or sleeping. I don't see how he could sit a horse."

When they got to Jim, he was still out of it, so they got busy building a travois for him. Robert wasn't much help, but he stuck with Vicki doing his best to comfort her, he thought. She was so glad to see them that she didn't notice how possessive he was.

When the travois was completed and covered with Jim's bedroll, he was gently lifted onto it and strapped down. One of the men saddled the horses, and when they were ready to head home, Robert suggested Vicki could ride with him. She politely declined and mounted one of Jim's horses, which didn't sit too well with Robert, and he sulked until they reached her house.

The ride took the rest of the day, and they reached Vicki's house just as the sun set. Her mother and several neighbor ladies ran to meet them.

Robert rushed to lift her from the horse, but she pushed him away and ran to her mother, where they embraced and cried for a long time. The mother constantly asked, "Are you hurt? Did they harm you? Are you okay, Vicki? Talk to me, did they....?"

"No, Mom, I'm fine. Jim got there just in time. He killed one, but he was shot and needs a doctor."

Mom took over at that point, "Bring him on inside," she said as she held the door open for them. "Put him in Vicki's bed, and one of you go for the doctor."

A man had each corner of the travois as they gently carried him into the house.

Robert suggested, "Wouldn't he be better off at the doctor's office where he can take care of him?"

"No, he'll be better off here, the doctor doesn't have a nurse, and he's going to need a lot of nursing." Robert certainly didn't want to hear that.

Vicki led them to her room and turned the covers down on the bed.

Robert stood nearby watching and didn't like how this turned out, so he stomped away with his head hanging.

Vicki didn't notice any of that, but her mother did, "I'm afraid you hurt Robert's feelings. I think he's jealous."

"So what? He'll get over it. Mom, you should have seen him. He was so brave. Even after he was shot, he didn't give up. He kept coming until he killed one of them and ran the other one away. I feared he would die and didn't know what to do for him."

"Well, it looks like you did a good job. Now you rest while I fix you a good hot bath and get you a change of clothes. You look a fright."

Mom got busy preparing the bath and fixing a meal for Vicki and herself. When the bath was ready, she called Vicki, "Your bath is ready. When you finish, I'll have your supper ready. Vicki, did you hear me?" There was no answer, so she looked in her room and found Vicki asleep across the foot of the bed.

She smiled, got a blanket, covered both of them, and let them sleep.

The doctor showed up a few minutes later and quietly examined Jim, changed his bandages, and said it looked like he should make a full recovery. "It doesn't look like the bullets hit any main arteries, so if he doesn't get an infection, he should be fine in a few days. What about Vicki, was she…?"

"She said she wasn't, so let's take her word for it, okay?"

"Okay, but keep a close eye on her. If she starts showing any unusual behavior, you let me know."

"Thank you, Doctor."

"I'll leave this bottle of pain medicine if he wakes up and needs it, which he probably will. The directions are on the bottle. I'll stop by tomorrow and check on both of them."

"Thanks, Doctor."

The bath and the food were cold when Vicki finally awoke. She sat up on the bed and looked around. Her mother was sitting beside the bed, knitting.

"What time is it? How long have I been asleep?"

"It's almost time for breakfast. You've been asleep for almost ten hours."

"How is he? Has he been awake at all?"

"He woke up a couple of times, was very restless and in pain. I gave him a little water and got him to take a few spoons of broth, and then he went right back to sleep."

"Did he say anything?"

"He just wanted to know where he was and what happened. And then he asked about you. He wanted to know where you were. I pointed to you, sleeping at his feet. It looked like he tried to smile, but he was asleep before he could get it done."

"Mom, I'm gonna marry that man."

"Vicki, you don't even know him. He may be an outlaw himself, for all you know. You've only known him, what, three days, and he's been asleep most of that time."

"I know enough about him to know he's a good man. That's all I need to know."

"What if he's already married?"

"Oh." Her hand went to her mouth. "No, he can't be."

"Well, probably not, but there is that possibility. You better not get too attached until you know more about him. I don't want to see you get hurt."

"Okay, Mom."

They made sure Jim was tucked into bed nice and comfortable, and then they both went to bed in Mom's room. Vicki lay awake most of the night thinking about Jim and what her mom had said. Twice she sneaked out of bed and stood by Jim as he slept. A lamp was burning low on a chest across the room. As Vicki stood by the bed, she saw Jim's clothes lying across a chair where the doctor had left them. She slowly picked up the shirt and examined the contents of the pockets. She removed a folded piece of paper and got the shock of her life. There was the wanted poster accusing him of murder. Her life seemed to fall apart in that instant. She let out a tiny scream, and her mother came running. When she saw the look on Vicki's face, she knew something terrible had happened. Her first thought was that Jim had died. But then she saw Vicki staring at the piece of paper. She gently removed it from Vicki's hand and read it. She put her arm around Vicki, drew her close, and hugged her. Vicki was crying uncontrollably while her mom tried to get her to return to bed. Vicki was having none of that. "There has to be a mistake, Mom. I know he could never murder anyone. Maybe he killed someone, but I know it couldn't be murder. I won't believe it until he tells me he did it."

"Come back to bed, Vicki. You're just tired. You've been through a lot the last couple of days. When he wakes up, we'll ask him about it. If he's the gentleman you think he is, he'll tell us how that came about."

Vicki laid the wanted poster on the side table, returned to her mother's room, and got back in bed, but there was no sleep for her the rest of the night.

She was back in Jim's room bright and early the next morning. Jim was showing signs of coming around, but he was still unaware of his sur-roundings. Vicki went to the kitchen and returned with a small bowl of soup. She gently attempted to awaken him. After a few tries, he opened his eyes and looked around the room. When he saw Vicki, his eyes lit up, and it looked like he tried to smile, but it didn't quite reach his eyes. He just lay there staring at her. She placed her hand on his cheek and asked if he wanted something to eat. He tried to speak, but only a whisper growl came out. He tried again, "Where am I?"

"You are in my house; I'm back home, thanks to you. How do you feel?"

"I don't know. I feel sore all over. What happened?"

Vicki paused a moment before answering, "You don't remember?"

"No, I don't remember much of anything, but I remember you. You're the prettiest girl I ever saw."

She blushed and said, "Thank you, Jim, and I think you're the most handsome man I have ever met."

He reached for her hand but grimaced in pain and asked, "What happened? Why am I here?"

"Jim, you were shot twice. Don't you remember, I was kidnapped, and you came to rescue me? One of the kidnappers shot you, and you shot him. That's how you were able to save me."

"I saved you?"

"Yes, you did. And then some men from town came looking for me and brought us back here. This is where I live with my mom."

"Oh, yeah, I remember your mom. She's almost as pretty as you. That's obviously where you get your good looks."

"Jim, you're embarrassing me."

"Get used to it."

"Do you feel like eating some soup?"

"I do feel hungry. Maybe I can eat some. I'll try."

"Let's see if we can set you up some."

She called her mom, and the two of them were able to raise him enough to get a couple of pillows behind him.

She retrieved the soup from the side table and spoon-fed him all he could eat. A few minutes later, he was dozing off again. She pulled the blanket over him and left him to get his rest. The wanted poster was still on the table beside the bed, but she didn't have the heart to ask him about it. Maybe when he was feeling better.

CHAPTER 9

Jim slept the night through but was awake when Vicki came into his room to check on him the next morning. He was feeling much better but very sore in his left arm and right shoulder. He could move the right arm, but if he tried to move the shoulder, he paid the price of excruciating pain, so he only tried that once.

Vicki brought coffee and more broth, sat by his bed, and helped him eat and drink until she had to leave for the café with her mom. She told him she would be gone most of the day but would come home to check on him when she could get away.

"That shouldn't be necessary," he said, "but it will be nice to see you."

"Is there anything I can get you before I leave?"

"If you will bring my gun and gun belt over here, just hang it on the bedpost."

"Why do you want your gun?"

"I would feel more comfortable if it's where I can reach it since I'm going to be here alone. You never know when you might need it."

She retrieved the gun from the chair across the room and hung it on the bedpost within his reach.

She thought about the wanted poster and almost asked him about it but decided to wait until later when they had more time to discuss it if he would even talk about it.

She was about to leave the room when he decided to try to get out of bed and sit up for a while. She came back to the bed to help him. He threw the covers back and started to put his feet on the floor when he suddenly jerked the covers back over him and asked, "Where are my clothes? Who took my clothes? I'm... I don't have any clothes on."

Vicki saw his face and his reaction and couldn't keep from laughing. "Mom took your clothes so she could wash them. They are right here on the chair. Do you want me to help you get dressed?" She was still laughing as his face got redder and redder.

"No, but thank you, I can manage it."

"Are you sure you don't need any help?" She asked with a devilish expression and a chuckle. "I better wait here in case you need help."

"No, your mom needs your help more; you better go with her."

She was still laughing when she left the room.

When he was sure everyone was out of the house, he attempted to sit on the side of the bed and get his underwear and pants on, but his arm and shoulder gave him so much pain he decided to wait until later. He gently lay back on the bed, pulled the covers over him, and was asleep in a few minutes.

Vicki and her mother left the house, went to the café, and got ready for the breakfast crowd they could always depend on. Vicki was waiting tables, her mom was in the kitchen, and both were so busy they had no time to do more than be friendly with everyone who came in. They knew everyone and what they would order when they came in the door.

One of the customers was Robert Freeman. He came in almost every morning to flirt with Vicki. This morning he was exceptionally pushy, trying to get Vicki's attention, but she was too busy to talk to him. She brought his coffee, took his order, and left to take it to her mom in the kitchen. When she returned with his food, he asked her, with a smirk,

"How is your patient doing? Is he getting all the care and attention he needs while lying in your bed?"

"Yes, he is. I'll tell him you were asking about him. I'm sure he'll be pleased to know you care." She hurried away to take care of another customer, "Hey, don't walk away when I'm talking to you."

"Robert, can't you see I'm swamped? I don't have time to stand here talking to you. I have customers waiting for their food."

"Yeah, there's always something, ain't it?"

As she walked away, he said, "I think I'll go by and see how the patient is doing. He may need help getting to the outhouse or something." He laughed at his joke, dropped some change on the table, and left.

Vicki rushed back, grabbed him by the arm, and pulled him around to face her, "Don't you dare go over there and cause trouble, Robert Freeman. I'll never speak to you again if you do. Do you hear me?"

Robert laughed as he left and walked toward Vicki's house. She watched him and cursed under her breath but knew nothing she could do about it. If he went to her house and confronted Jim, there would be trouble, and Jim was in no condition to defend himself. He couldn't even get out of bed without help. She ran to the kitchen to tell her mom what Robert was planning, but Mom was too busy getting orders ready to listen to her. She returned to the dining room and continued taking orders, cleaning tables, and carrying the dirty dishes to the kitchen to wash later, but her mind was on what Robert said he would do. She hurried through her chores until she could leave and check on Jim, but it seemed that today was one of those days when everyone in town came in to eat, hang around, and visit and always wanted more coffee and dessert. She was so flustered her mom called her to the kitchen to ask what was going on. When Mom heard what Robert was planning, she told Vicki, "You stay here. I don't want you getting mixed up in that. If you went over there now, you could get hurt. Jim will have to take care of himself."

"But Mom, he's hurt; he can't even get out of bed."

Mom said, "I don't think Robert has the guts to tackle anyone to their face. Jim will be fine. You wait and see."

"I hope you're right, Mom."

Jim awakened about mid-morning and lay in bed thinking about his situation. He could hardly move his arms enough to feed himself. He had not tried to get dressed but was pretty sure that would not go so well, but he was considering attempting it. He didn't want to lie in bed all the time and have Vicki and her mom waiting on him, hand and foot. His clothes were well out of his reach on a chair at the foot of the bed. He would have to get out of bed, walk around to the end of the bed to get to them, and then struggle to get into them. When he realized he was completely naked under the covers, he had second thoughts about getting out of bed. What if Vicki came to check on him before he could get dressed? That would be too embarrassing to bear. While considering what he should do, the front door opened, and heavy footsteps entered the house. He looked around for someplace to hide, but there was no time for that. He remembered his gun belt hanging on the headboard. He reached for it with his left hand and was painfully reminded of his wounds. He gasped with pain and slowly crumpled back onto the bed, but he knew he had to get that gun. He attempted to reach it again, this time using his right hand. It was still painful and seemed to take forever just to get his hand up to where he could get a grip on the pistol. He took a firm hold and slowly began lifting it from the holster. He didn't think he could do it, but at the last second, just before he had to drop it back into the holster, it came clear, and his hand and arm dropped down to the bed. He still held the gun and slipped it under the cover just as a man stepped into the room. He stopped just inside the door and saw Jim lying in bed with a blanket pulled up to his chin.

The two men stared at each other until Jim asked, "Who are you, and what do you want?"

"Oh, I just came to check on you, to see how you are doing laying up in my girl's bed all nice and comfortable. I think it's time you were up and out of here. I don't want you hanging around."

Jim gave the man a hard stare for a full minute before he answered, "Is this your house?"

The man hesitated a moment and then stuttered, "n n o, but I'm gonna help you leave just the same."

Jim gave him a smirk of a smile and said, "Well, whoever you are, I don't like your attitude, and also, I don't think you are man enough to make me leave until I get good and ready. So turn around a leave before you bite off more than you can chew."

Robert moved closer to the side of the bed and looked down at Jim, apparently helpless, "You talk big for a man who can't even get out of bed. I'll help you with that." He reached for Jim to pull him out of bed. When he jerked the blanket back, he was looking down the barrel of a .44 revolver. His face suddenly turned white, and he jumped back like he had seen a rattler.

Jim slowly pulled the hammer back, letting it click loudly as it turned the cylinder. Robert was staring at the gun as he backed across the room with his hands in the air. "Don't shoot, I was just kidding with you. I wasn't gonna do anything."

"I know you weren't, and I'm just kidding with you. Now get out of this house, and don't you ever come around here again unless Vicki or her mom invite you, and they better be here when you come. Have I made myself clear enough, or do I need to make it clearer?" He said as he raised the revolver and pointed it directly at Robert's face.

With his hands still in the air, Robert rapidly backed toward the door, "No, I understand. I'm leaving." Jim heard him rapidly leave the house, the front door slammed, and all was quiet.

Jim laid back and relaxed and thought about what had just happened. He had to laugh when he thought back to the expression on the man's face when he saw the gun.

He rested for a few minutes and decided it was time to get dressed. He slowly sat up, put his feet on the floor, placed the revolver on the night table, and saw the wanted poster. "Oh, no, now I have some explaining to do." He considered leaving before Vicki and her mom got home but reconsidered, knowing that would be very rude after all they had done for him. They deserved an explanation, and he didn't murder that man; it was an accident. A simple bar-room fight went wrong, and the dead man started it. What was he supposed to do, stand there and get beaten to a pulp by some bully? No, he had to set this straight somehow. He didn't intend to go through life with every lawman and bounty hunter looking to put a bullet in him for the reward money.

He slowly worked his way to his clothes and struggled to get into them, hoping no one would come in before he was fully dressed. He had to sit and rest several times, but he finally got it done.

With his gun belt strapped around his waist, he felt much more comfortable as he made his way to the kitchen to find something to eat.

He went for the coffee first. When it was on the stove and beginning to hiss, the back door burst open. He spun around and dropped to one knee as he pulled his pistol, cocked the hammer back, and aimed at the person coming in the door.

Vicki screamed and jumped back, hit the door, and banged it against the wall, making an awful noise. That scared her even more, and Jim was still trying to decipher what was happening when he recognized Vicki standing against the wall, scared half to death.

"Oh, Lord Vicki, you scared me. I almost shot you!"

Vicki stared at him for a moment and sank to the floor. Jim thought she had fainted and rushed to her side. He dropped to the floor beside her, pulled her close, held her, and apologized over and over for scaring her. She was still in shock when Jim lifted her chin and kissed her on the lips, "I'm so sorry. I thought you were that man coming back."

"Robert was here?"

"I don't know who he was. He barged in here and told me to leave. I convinced him I would only leave when you told me to leave."

She was lying relaxed in his arms and seemed to be enjoying it. "In that case, you may be here a long time." She pulled his face down to hers and kissed him until they had to come up for air.

That's when he realized he was in pain and attempted to extract himself from Vicki. She saw the pain in his face and helped him to his feet and onto a chair.

The coffee pot was boiling on the stove, and the aroma penetrated their senses, "Let me get you some coffee," she said, "you sit here and rest."

She brought a cup for each of them, and they sat sipping and staring into each other's eyes until she said, "Don't look at me like that. You're embarrassing me."

"I can't help myself; you're so beautiful. You have the most beautiful eyes I have ever seen." Finally, he cleared his throat and said, "I have something I need to tell you."

"Okay, I think I know what it is, but go ahead and tell me."

CHAPTER 10

"**I** know you saw the wanted poster, and I need to explain how that happened."

"Okay, I'm listening. This better be good."

"I don't know if you'll consider it good or not, but it's the truth."

He told about the barroom fight and how the man was still alive when he left the bar. "I don't know what happened after I left, but I didn't murder that man. He started the fight, and I only hit him two or three times. For all I know, someone else could have killed him after I left. But I don't know what I can do to clear my name. But as long as those wanted posters are circulating, every lawman and bounty hunter in the country will be after my hide."

"Oh, Jim, what if you went back and explained what happened, maybe they would believe you, and you said some men saw the whole thing. Surely they will tell what happened."

"But what happens if I go back and explain and they don't believe me? They'll just hang me and forget about it. I can't do that. I have to think of a better way or leave the country."

"Oh no, I don't want you to leave. We'll think of something."

He took her hand, looked into her eyes again, and said, "I have a brother in Texas who has been after me to come down there. We could go there, get married, and they will never know where I am."

"But Jim, there will always be that murder charge hanging over your head. Could we live like that, knowing a lawman might show up at the door at any time to arrest you and bring you back here to stand trial, or some bounty hunter will try to collect the bounty? I don't want to start our life together like that, do you?"

"No, but I don't know what else I can do, do you?"

"No, but there has to be a way, and we don't have to make that decision now anyway. Let's think about it while you get well. We'll come up with something. If we don't, I'll go to Texas with you, and we'll face it together."

He pulled her to him in a tight hug, and they remained like that until they heard horses galloping toward them from the street.

Jim jumped to his feet, grimacing in pain, "I don't like the sound of that. I'm going out the back door, and you see who that is. I'll be in the barn." He was out the door in a flash and deep in the barn, looking out from far back where no one could see him from outside. He heard Vicki when she opened the door and scream, "What are you doing? You can't barge in here like that. Get out."

"We're here for that murderer. Where is he?"

"I don't know what you're talking about. There's no murderer here. Now get out."

"We're not leaving without that killer; now get out of the way."

There was a scream, "Stop it, get your hands off me."

Jim heard all this and was ready to charge into the house, but there were too many to take on alone, and he would only get killed. That would play right into their hands and do Vicki no good at all. He was in a dilemma as to what to do. That was settled for him when he heard one of the men tell the others, "I'll check the barn, the rest of you check the house, don't forget the attic."

Jim didn't have time to escape, so he quickly looked around for a place to hide. His two horses standing in stalls would be a dead giveaway that he was still there. He had to think of something else quickly. He didn't have time to climb to the loft, and then he remembered when he came into the barn, he was almost blind for a few seconds until his eyes adjusted to the dim interior after being in the bright sunlight outside. He ran to the side of the barn door and flattened his back against the front wall. He heard the man approaching and was ready when he stepped through the door. Jim stuck the pistol in his back and said, "Howdy, Robert, you looking for something?"

Robert turned toward the voice, but Jim said, "NO! Don't turn around; drop that gun, or I'll drop you."

The man hesitated a moment, then slowly lowered his arm and dropped the pistol.

"That was smart. Now please do me a favor. Do you see that buckskin in the second stall? You will put that saddle on him and cinch it down tight. Then you will put the pack saddle on the other one. You won't get hurt if you do it nicely, quietly, and quickly. If you don't do exactly as I tell you, I will not be responsible for what happens to you. Now get moving and be quick about it."

Jim watched the man go about saddling the horses while keeping a close watch on the house in case someone came to check on their friend. He seemed to be taking a long time getting the job done, and Jim kept telling him to hurry it up, but it didn't seem to do any good. The man delayed as long as he could, hoping someone would come looking for him. Vicki was still screaming at the men to get out and leave her alone, but they paid no attention to her and kept searching the house. It wasn't that big, and Jim couldn't imagine what was taking them so long but was glad they were occupied.

The horses were finally ready, and Jim mounted the buckskin and took the lead rope on the pack horse, "Okay, Robert, you lead the way out the back door, and don't do anything stupid. I don't want to kill you, but I will if you don't do what I tell you. Walk out the door and continue straight until I tell you differently."

Robert looked around, hoping to see his friends coming, but they were still busy in the house. He took his time walking away with Jim riding behind, pushing him along.

"How far are you taking me?" Robert asked.

"Oh, I don't know, but considering what you had planned for me, we might keep walking the rest of the day."

"You better get your jollies while you can because when I get my hands on you, it's not going to be pretty."

"Well," Jim chuckled, "that gives me some ideas about what I can do with you."

"I have friends who will be looking for me, and when they catch up to us, you're going to be a dead man."

"Now, Robert, this is the second time you've tried to take advantage of me, and both times you've come out on the short end of it. Are you sure you want to keep trying? Your track record is not very good so far."

Robert had nothing to say for a few minutes. Jim kept a sharp watch behind them, but no activity indicated no one was following them. Jim chuckled loud enough for Robert to hear him, "It looks like your so-called friends aren't too anxious to help you out of the jam you got yourself in. Maybe you should look for better friends if you live long enough."

"Don't you worry about my friends. They'll take care of you in due time."

"I guess that remains to be seen. But you probably won't be around to see what happens."

"So what does that mean," Robert asked, "are you taking me out in the hills to kill me?"

"I guess that depends on you," Jim answered, "If you do what I tell you and don't cause me any problems, you may get to see another day. I don't know why I would even consider doing that, knowing what you planned to do to me. What do you think I should do with you?"

Robert didn't have an answer, so he continued to stumble along, getting slower and slower. Jim could tell Robert's feet were hurting him. Walking in riding high-heel boots was not something anyone wanted to do if there were other options.

After another quarter mile, Robert had had enough. He stopped in the middle of the trail and turned to face Jim, "This is as far as I go. If you're gonna kill me, then kill me and get it over with. I'm not taking another step."

Jim pointed his horse straight at Robert and pushed him along in front of him. Robert staggered, trying to maintain his balance, knowing the horse would walk all over him if he fell. Jim touched his horse with his heels lightly, and the horse continued to press forward. Robert continued to fall back until he decided to move on his own before something worse happened. He turned and ran a few steps to get away from the horse.

Jim checked behind him, saw no sign of pursuit, and decided he had taken this far enough.

"Okay, Robert, you can stop now. Sit down and take your boots off."

"Are you crazy? I'm not taking my boots off for you are anyone else."

"Okay, remember what I told you. You might live to see another day if you didn't give me trouble. Do you remember that? Well, you are giving me trouble, so the other option is I shoot you, and you can keep your boots. But the choice is yours. Make up your mind." Jim pulled his revolver from the holster and cocked the hammer back as Robert stared at him in shock. Slowly he lowered himself to the ground and removed his boots.

"Hand them to me, and don't try anything funny. You're not out of this yet."

Robert carefully handed the boots to Jim. Jim's pistol was looking him straight in the eye as he reached the boots up to him.

Jim took the boots, "Start walking back to your devoted friends. I'm sure they are searching everywhere for you. You don't want to keep them waiting."

Robert nervously eased away down the trail like he was expecting a bullet in the back at any moment.

Jim waited until he was thirty feet away, then turned his horse and rode up the trail at an easy gallop with the pack horse following on a short lead. He had no idea what Robert's friends were doing or how long it would take them to find him, but he was not going to wait around to find out.

He kept to the trail until another one cut off to the south. He didn't know where it would take him, but then he didn't know where the one he was on would take him. He knew nothing about this part of the country, so he would have to play everything by ear. He knew they had been heading northeast since they left Vicki's house, the new trail was cutting back to the south at this point, but there was no telling which way it would end up. It didn't matter; all he was interested in right now was putting some distance between himself and Robert's gang of bounty hunters.

He was so tense during his escape he didn't notice the pain in his arm and shoulder until he was half a mile up the trail. He suddenly felt weak and slightly nauseous and had to stop for a few minutes. He turned his horse off the trail into the thicker brush on the side of a steep hill until he came to a large tree giving off a lot of shade. He took a long drink from his canteen and sat for a few minutes, gathering his strength until he felt strong enough to ease himself to the ground. Once he was sitting leaning back against the tree, he checked his wounds to see if they were bleeding. After a brief look, he was glad to see only a small amount of blood had seeped out of the shoulder wound, but it didn't appear to be a major problem at this point.

He had not tried to hide his trail since he didn't know he would be sitting here resting while his pursuers could be getting closer all the time. But once he thought about that, he began thinking about what he had done before reaching this spot. His head was not clear enough to re-think all the detail, but he knew he could be in trouble if anyone were close on his trail. He had to move, hide his tracks, and find a place to lay up for a few days until the pressure was off and his wounds had healed. Then he would go back to see Vicki and let her know he was safe. Then they would decide what to do next. Then he had a frightening thought, what if Vicki didn't want anything to do with him? Maybe he was taking too much for granted. That put him thinking about all they had said to each other. Had she made any commitment to him? Had he committed to her? His brain was not working very well, but he was now worried that she would write him off as a lost cause and go about her business. After all, they had only known each other a few days, and he was out of it most of that time. How did she really feel about him? Did she believe he was a murderer? He had to get back to her as soon as possible and get answers to all his questions. He had very strong feelings for her, but now he was having doubts about how she felt toward him. As worried as he was, he knew he had to get some rest, but he couldn't stay here.

A few more minutes, a few more drinks from the canteen, and he felt like he could ride. He got to his feet by holding onto the tree until he felt steady enough to walk. His horse stood while Jim struggled to pull himself onto the saddle. Once he was mounted, he didn't know which way to go. He decided to stay off the trail, if he could, and try to work his way back to the southwest. Somewhere along the way, he hoped to find a suitable place to hold up for a few days until he regained his strength.

His horses were well-rested and were raised in the Clinch Mountains of Tennessee, so they had no trouble navigating the terrain through these mountains. They took the ups and downs, creek crossings, and tight, narrow canyons like it happened every day. Nothing seemed to bother them.

Jim was constantly watching for someplace to hold up, so when they came to a stream gushing out of a narrow gouge in the side of a mountain, he turned his horse up the stream, not knowing how far it would take him, but he was getting desperate with night coming on fast in these mountains. The stream was littered with rocks and boulders. His horse maneuvered around them with ease, all the time remaining in the water, leaving no trail for anyone to follow.

CHAPTER 11

The canyon the creek flowed through was so narrow that Jim's feet touched each side of the walls that towered hundreds of feet above them. Echoes bounced off the walls several times as they drifted up and down the canyon. Jim became concerned about a possible flash flood coming down this canyon if there had been heavy rain in the higher country. He had not seen anything to make him think that would happen, but it was something to keep in mind if he would be in this canyon much longer.

He guessed he had gone over a mile and had not seen any way to get out. The water was from one to three feet deep and very swift in the narrow places and slower and shallower in the broader areas where the canyon walls were farther apart.

It was getting darker at the bottom of the canyon. The walls were so tall and close together that the only light coming in was from directly overhead. Jim's only choice was to keep going and hope a path presented itself before it was too dark to see.

His horses were tired from fighting the water for so long. They were less eager to challenge the waterfalls and the deeper pools. Jim knew he had to do something soon. He had seen no place to stop where they could get out of the water, nor any place where they could leave the canyon. He was afraid he would not be able to continue when it became too dark to see what was before them. He could trust his horses to a certain extent, knowing they had much better night vision than he did. But when it was totally dark, would the horse be able to see anything?

They had no choice but to continue. He had come too far to turn back, so he pressed on.

When it was almost too dark to see anything, he heard a different noise bouncing off the walls. He couldn't identify what it was. It didn't sound like a waterfall, and as they got closer, it became more confusing. It sounded like a waterfall, but then it didn't. He continued cautiously because he had no other choice.

The noise picked up just before he rounded a curve and saw the canyon completely blocked by a rock slide. The water was working its way around and between the large rocks, but he could see no way for a horse to get through. His vision was limited due to darkness. All he could see was a wall in front of him with water gushing through the seams. He sat cursing his luck for getting in this fix.

He sat looking at the dam, letting his horses catch their breath. After a few minutes, his horse started on his own volition. Jim didn't know where he was going since he saw no opening the way he was going. After only a few steps, he leaped to a higher level, took a few steps, and then another small leap to another higher level. A tug on the lead rope reminded him of the pack horse. He looked back and saw him hesitate a moment as if to say, "You sure you want to go there?" The horse took a deep breath and leaped, following his buddy.

Jim could see nothing but the walls on each side. They were close enough to touch with both feet if he didn't hold them in close to his horse. A few more lunges up a sharp incline, a few short turns to the right and left, more climbing and turns, and the horse had to stop for a breather.

He almost acted like he had been here before and knew where he was going. Jim knew that could not be the case since he had raised these horses from babies and knew where they had spent their entire lives. Could he have inherited that knowledge from some ancestor? He didn't know if such a thing was possible, but this horse definitely seemed to know where he was going and what was waiting for them.

After a few minutes of rest, he took a couple of deep breaths and proceeded to climb the mountain. Jim was at his horses' mercy. He could see nothing, so he held on and let his horse pick his way.

After what seemed like an hour, but probably was no more than fifteen minutes, the horse stopped, and then with a big lunge and a lot of scrambling for footage, he walked out on a flat surface, stopped, took a deep breath, and shook like a dog coming out of water.

Jim looked around in surprise. Sitting on a mountaintop, he could see at least a half mile. With the moon almost full, it was almost like full daylight.

He thought about fire and coffee, but before he unsaddled his horses, he needed to find a better place to settle down. His wounds hurt something awful, but he knew he would be here for a while once he removed the saddle and packs. He would never be able to get them back on the horse until he was much improved.

The top of the mesa where he was sitting was bare of trees and brush. Only a thin layer of soil supported scattered bunches of what looked like bunch-grass. There wasn't much of it, but at least the horses would have something to graze on.

Something was sticking up in the distance that might be trees or cliffs. When his horses rested a few more minutes, he touched his heels to his sides and rode toward the object, whatever it was. A little farther along, the ground dropped a few feet, and Jim looked at a small lake of several acres. Just on the other side of the lake was a grove of trees that should be a good place to set up camp.

There was plenty of dead wood for a fire and trees for shade, and he saw plenty of deer tracks around the water, so he would have no meat shortage.

He stepped down from the saddle, gave his big horse a pat on the neck, loosened the girth, and let the saddle fall to the ground. He removed the pack from the other horse and hobbled them so they wouldn't stray very far. He gave them a brief rub down and started gathering material for a fire, but he was so tired he decided to wait until he could see what he had to work with.

He spread his blankets, found a pack of jerky, chewed on it until his jaws were tired, curled up with his hat over his face, and tried to sleep, but the pain in his arm and shoulder wouldn't let him. He tried several different positions, but nothing worked. The wound on his right shoulder and left arm prevented him from lying on either side. After tossing and turning for over an hour, he was too tired to remain awake.

He finally drifted into a restless sleep filled with dreams of two beautiful women fighting over him in a bar. One hit the other with a bottle. She fell to the floor with blood pouring from her mouth and died. Jim came awake with a lunge, but pain shot through him. He let out a loud groan and sank back on his blankets. After a few minutes, he took a sip of water from his canteen and looked around his new camp.

The sun was just about to peak over the mountain to the east, and he realized he was hungry. He couldn't remember the last time he ate. The sticks he gathered the night before were still lying where he had left them, so he stuck a match to them and soon had a fire going with his coffee perking. When it was ready, he poured a cup and strolled to the edge of the trees to look around. The lake was only thirty feet away, with trees and brush growing right up to the edge. As he looked across the water, he saw several fish jump and knew he wouldn't have any trouble catching enough for a good meal. All he had to do was find a suitable pole, rig a hook, catch a few grasshoppers, and he would have a nice fish dinner.

It turned out to be a lot harder than it looked. The pole would not be a problem, but he still had no string or hook. He searched his saddlebags and packs but found nothing he could use. He poured another coffee and sat in the shade, chewing on jerky and thinking.

The fish were jumping like they were inviting him to come and catch them. The more jerky he ate, the more determined he was to catch fish and kill a deer as soon as one presented itself. He didn't have to wait very long. Before he finished his second cup of coffee, he saw movement in the trees at the end of the lake not over fifty yards away. A large doe and two smaller deer came from the trees, walked to the water's edge, and started drinking. They didn't seem to know he was there, or they had no fear of him if they did know. Being this far from civilization, they probably had never seen a man before, and what little wind there was blew from them toward Jim so they wouldn't catch his scent. He sat in the shade and watched them get their water, and the smaller ones began to frolic in the sun. Jim reached for his rifle, which was still in the scabbard on his saddle, took hold, and pulled, and pain shot through his shoulder; he turned loose of the rifle and gasped for breath until the pain subsided. That was enough to make him decide to wait a while to kill a deer. He realized he would never be able to get it skinned and back to his camp in his condition. That left fishing as his best solution for food. But he had no fishing line, fish hook, or bait. That didn't seem to have been a problem for the early settlers who came to this country with nothing except the clothes on their back. And the clothes they made from the raw material they found when they arrived here.

Jim thought about that as he chewed another piece of jerky and drank his coffee. The more he chewed, the more determined he was to make it happen.

He looked around the area he had chosen for his home until he died or got well enough to ride out of there. His wounds seemed to be healing well enough but were still too sore for him to do any lifting, like putting the saddle back on his horse, so he would be here for a while.

He sat and thought and came up with a solution for getting the deer. But that would have to wait another day while he got his plan finalized and healed more.

In the meantime, he started working on a plan to catch fish. The fishing pole wouldn't be a problem. There were enough slender saplings around the pond to give him a choice. The fishing line and hook were going to be the problem. Maybe a fish trap would work until he could get that worked out. He had made fish traps since he was a kid. All it took was a bunch of slender branches, weeds, anything he could weave together. He spent the rest of the day gathering the supplies and putting his trap together. It wasn't exactly what he had hoped for, but before he finished it, his arm and shoulder were hurting so bad he was willing to settle for what he had. He held it up, looked at his finished product, and decided it would have to do.

With his boots and socks removed and his pants rolled above his knees, he dragged the trap to the water's edge. The first step into the water brought a gasp from him. He had never felt water so cold. He stepped back and thought about this some more. After some thought, he decided there was no other way, so he took that first step again. This time, knowing what to expect, he wasn't surprised, so he took the second and third steps until he was up to his knees in the ice-cold water. He would like to have gotten the trap into deeper water, but this would have to do for now. Maybe he could come up with a better solution later.

He placed a rock on top to hold it down, returned to shore, and hoped it worked. He had tied one end of his rope to the trap to pull it out without getting wet again.

He returned to his campfire and poured another cup of coffee. "This will get very boring if it goes on for very long."

His horses were grazing by the lake and seemed perfectly content with their situation. Well, why not, they had plenty of fresh water and all the grass they could eat, and they didn't have to do anything to earn it. Wouldn't it be nice if his life was that simple?

He took a sip of coffee and discovered it was already cold. He started to throw it out, but on second thought, he poured it back into the pot to reheat. If he were to be here for more than a few days, he would need every ounce of supplies he brought in.

After sitting in the shade for an hour, he became bored and decided to explore his mountaintop mesa. He gently removed his rifle from the saddle scabbard, strapped on his gun belt, and started slowly strolling around the lake toward the rise in ground to his right. To his left was the open, bare table top with the lake in the middle, but to the right was a rise of ground, and he wanted to see what was there. As he strolled, he noticed the tracks around the lake's edge. The tracks of the three deer that came out for water early this morning were there, but there were also tracks of a bear, and at one point farther along, he found tracks of what he thought was a mountain lion. He would have to keep a sharp eye on his horses. He didn't know if a cougar, or mountain lion, would attack something as large as a horse, but he was pretty sure that a bear would.

From the number of tracks, he knew this was a popular watering hole for the animals in the area. Deer tracks were numerous, but the bear tracks were thick enough to cause concern. He didn't want to come face to face with a full-grown bear. A bullet from the rifle he was carrying would have to hit just the right spot to drop him before it got to him. The scoop around these parts was that the black bear that occupied these mountains were usually not aggressive toward humans unless they had cubs with them, and then they would take on anything to protect their young.

The edge of the mesa dropped off to the valley below. Trees and underbrush were thick with large pines that would take several people to reach around them.

As he continued around the lake at the mesa's edge, he found a trail that dropped over the edge. It was pretty steep, and he wasn't sure he wanted to risk it at this time. It appeared to wind around the trees and boulders as it descended to a lower level. More large boulders were piled on top of other boulders, creating a maze. His curiosity got the better of him. He had to see what was in that mess of rocks. As he cautiously crept down the trail, he thought this would be a perfect place for a bear to den up. He checked to make sure there was a round in the barrel of his rifle and loosened his pistol in the holster, knowing the guns would be useless against a full-grown bear, but it gave him a slight sense of security knowing it was there and ready.

He was checking the trail for tracks, but it was almost solid rock, so any tracks would not be visible. Droppings from deer, rabbits, and birds were plentiful, and a large pile of bear poop was right in front of him. He studied it for a moment and determined it was probably a couple of days old, making him feel better.

As he approached the pile of rocks, he saw a wide crack a man could squeeze through. He was ready for anything that might jump out at him as he slowly eased up to the opening. The first thing he noticed was no smell of wild animals or visible signs of traffic going in and out. He was feeling better about the situation already. As he entered the opening, he realized it was larger than it initially appeared. It was probably large enough to get his horses in here. He stopped and listened. It was too dark back there to see how deep this hole went. There seemed to be a back wall blocking it, but as he got closer, an opening to the side gave access to another part of the cave, if that's what this was. He stepped around the boulder and came face to face with a solid wall. So this was the extent of the cave, and no animals lived there. There didn't appear to have been water standing or running through it. That's when he decided to move his gear here instead of building a shelter on top of the mesa. It would be a little walk to get water, but not enough of a problem to matter. The horses would still be on top and out of sight, but he should be able to hear them if they became frightened and put up a ruckus.

After a little more looking around, he returned to his camp and started gathering his gear. He could only carry a very small amount due to his injuries, but before sundown, he had everything moved into the cave. The saddle and packsaddle caused the most problem, but he solved that by attaching his rope to them, looping it around his horse's neck, and letting the horse drag them. The horses were then hobbled and turned loose on top of the mesa. With plenty of water and grass, they wouldn't stray very far.

He gathered dry wood from beneath the trees and soon had enough to last through the night in case the bear returned. He felt pretty sure the fire would keep it away.

He built a fire near the entrance and stashed his bedroll toward the back wall.

The fire was comforting to sit back, sip his coffee, and snack on jerky. Maybe tomorrow, he would have fish to eat. He realized he should have checked his trap before it got too dark, but he was too busy moving his camp and didn't think about it. That would be first on his list of things to do tomorrow.

CHAPTER 12

He was surprised the next morning when he awoke and realized he had gotten a pretty good night's sleep. He sat up, pushed his blanket off, stirred the coals from last night's fire, added more wood, put the coffee pot on, and walked to the entrance of his cave to see what was happening in his world today.

From where he stood, he could see for miles across the valley below. But he could only see about fifty feet in the other direction, up the hill toward the lake. He reached back for his rifle, climbed the trail, and looked across the lake and the surrounding mesa. His horses were grazing not far from where he had left them last night. That told him everything had been quiet during the night.

He thought about his fish trap and started to check it when he noticed movement in the trees near the lake. He squatted down with only his eyes and the top of his head above the rim and waited to see what it was. He was pretty sure it was the deer he saw yesterday morning. If it was, he would take one of the young ones. He didn't think he could take another day of jerky.

A minute passed before one of the young ones darted from the brush and headed for the water. Jim waited until mother and two offspring had their drink and were ready to head back into the bush. He drew a bead on one and dropped him. The other two disappeared back into the trees. Jim took his time getting it dressed, taking the best pieces of meat to be smoked and cured so it would last a while.

He cut the meat into small pieces because he couldn't carry anything heavy, but when he returned to his camp in the cave, he cut it into thin strips and hung it over the bed of coals. The juices dripped into the fire sending up an aroma that had his stomach growling. It was still dripping and sizzling when he had a strip in his hands, eating and drinking his coffee, thinking, "This is the life. Sure beats jerky every meal."

He was almost finished with his meal when he noticed the wind had picked up and the sky was getting dark. "It looks like we may have some bad weather coming. I better check on the horses and make sure they don't wander off." It was a common habit of talking to themselves that men got into when alone so much. He had not been alone that long, but the sound of a voice was comforting, even if it was his own.

He strapped on his pistol, picked up his rifle, and climbed the hill to look out over the flat top of the mesa. The horses stood side by side, head to tail, swishing flies off each other.

He took a moment to look over the mesa but didn't see anything to be concerned about except the weather. The horses didn't seem bothered since they lived outside in it every day. They were still wearing the hobbles, so they were not going anywhere quickly.

Jim took the last few steps, reached the top of the mesa, walked to the horses, spoke to each of them, and spent a few minutes petting them. An ear-piercing clap of thunder shattered the silence. It was so loud and unexpected that the horses jumped, and Jim staggered back and almost fell before he caught his balance and realized what it was. The sky was solid black now. The wind picked up and blew debris across the flat surface and into the lake. Jim calmed the horses, removed their hobbles, and led them to the drop-off above his cave. With a bit of coaxing, he got them down the steep trail. The opening to his cave was a tight squeeze for them, but they managed to work their way in, past his fire, and against the back wall. The fire near the entrance didn't leave much room for his bedroll, but he figured they would make do for one night. After a few minutes, they seemed content and glad to be out of the storm.

Within a few minutes, the rain was coming down in sheets, the wind whipped the trees about, and the day looked like night. Lightning lit up the sky, followed by ear-splitting thunder. Even in the cave and out of the storm, the horses became restless, and Jim was busy keeping them from bolting.

Rain blew in the entrance but didn't reach him, so after he got his horses settled down, he sat back and enjoyed the show, which lasted throughout the day.

Night came, and he tried to sleep, but his wounds still bothered him and prevented him from resting comfortably. There just wasn't any comfortable position. He tossed and tried to turn, but he hurt so much each time that it took several minutes to get back to sleep. When he knew he should be up and doing something in the morning, he was too tired to make an effort, but he hurt just from laying in the same position for so long.

The storm seemed to have passed over, as everything was quiet outside. It was light enough to make out the trees and the outline of the mountain in the distance. The horses were restless, so he struggled to his feet and looked outside. Everything was calm and peaceful, so he led the horses out, and they immediately charged up the steep incline and out onto the level surface by the lake. They got a drink first and then started grazing on the lush grass near the water's edge. They didn't seem the least interested in leaving this mountaintop, so he thought about not putting the hobbles on them today. But, before he made the final decision about

that, he walked around the entire edge of the mesa to see if there was another way down other than the way they came up. It only took about
thirty minutes to make the circle and was glad to see there didn't appear
to be another easy way down.

The first step down was at least ten feet; in other places, it was over
one hundred feet straight down. He checked the trail they used coming
up here and decided he could easily block it with a few limbs that had
fallen from nearby trees. That turned into a bigger job than he imagined.
Pain shot through his shoulder when he tried to pick up the first limb.
He gasped and dropped the limb, staggered back against the tree, and
stood groaning in pain until he recovered enough to continue. He decided right away he would use smaller limbs and brush. It would still take
him quite a while to gather enough to do the job. Not that it would take
a lot of brush, but he could only lift and carry small pieces.

With that decision made, he returned to his cave and made a breakfast of venison and coffee. That was his only choice, except for jerky and
coffee, and he had eaten enough to last a lifetime.

When he returned to finish closing off the trail, the horses were still
grazing near the lake. He completed the job in less than half an hour,
stood back, inspected his work, and decided it would have to do. They
had water and plenty of grass to last them until he was ready to leave here
if he didn't have any complications with his injuries.

That thought made him think that maybe he had better change the
bandages. It had been several days, and he had hurt himself a few times
and didn't know what kind of damage that might have done. He returned to his cave, removed the bandages, and inspected the two he could
see, his left arm and right shoulder. The arm was healing nicely, so he left
the bandage off to enjoy the open air. The right shoulder was another
story. It had broken open, and blood saturated the bandage. It appeared

to be slightly inflamed and was sore to the touch. That's what he could see in the front. In the back, where the bullet exited, was a mystery. He couldn't see or reach it, so he only hoped it wasn't any worse than the front. He sat by his fire, studying what he could do. He knew he needed to be treating it, but he had no medical supplies or knowledge other than what he had seen his mom and dad do when one of the kids injured themselves. That was usually only a minor scratch, not something as serious as a gunshot wound. His mom would pour coal oil on it, wrap a rag around it and tell him to go back to doing what got him hurt in the first place. He had to laugh when he thought about that. But, he and his brother and sister had grown strong and healthy. Now here he was with a murder charge hanging over him and two bullet holes in him.

After thinking it over, he only had water to treat his wounds, so he took his canteen to the lake, filled it with clean, cold water, and returned to the fire. Taking the small pot he used to heat his food, he rinsed it and filled it with water, and put it on the fire to heat. While it was heating, he looked through his packs, saddlebags, and pockets to see what he could find. He came up with a shirt that had been hauled around in his bag since he didn't know when, but it looked clean. He laid it aside to use as bandages if he could figure out how.

The water finally came to a boil. He watched it bubble for a couple of minutes and then sat it aside to cool. He wanted it hot, but not hot enough to burn his skin.

He sat back and thought over his situation. He didn't like anything about it. He had lost track of the one man responsible for killing his folks and burning his home. He had a murder charge against him, lawmen and bounty hunters after him, and two bullet holes causing him problems and getting worse; he was stuck out in nowhere, alone, and had no way to treat his wounds. Other than that, everything seemed to be going just great.

He tore a strip off the shirt, put it in hot water, and put the pot back on the fire to boil to help clean the shirt. After a couple of minutes, he removed it from the fire again and set it aside to cool. Meanwhile, he sat, considering his situation and trying to decide his options. He came up with many possibilities but turned them down, except maybe two or three. He decided he had no choice but to give up on catching his folk's killer. His top priorities now were to get well and clear his name of the murder charge. But how could he do that? He had no experience with such things. He only knew to attack it head-on and let the bodies lay where they fall.

The water was finally cool enough, so he lifted the cloth from the water, lay back against his bedroll, and applied it to his wounds. He gasped when the hot water hit his tender skin but held it there until it felt better and then dipped it in the pan and applied it again and again, alternating between the wounds. He kept that up until he grew tired, sat the pot aside, and rested. His injuries felt so much better after being bathed that he relaxed and fell asleep.

When he awoke, the sun was past the halfway mark toward its final resting place for the day. He felt much better and got up from his bed and walked outside. The sky was clear, with only a slight breeze blowing. He walked up the steep trail to check on his horses. When he stuck his head over the edge to look over the flat surface of the lake, he didn't see them. He walked out further and called but got no answer. A shot of fear went through him. If he was stranded here with no horse, he would have one heck of a time getting back to civilization.

The first thing he thought of was the top of the trail that he had blocked off. He did his best to hurry over and check if they had pushed their way through. When he arrived, the brush and tree limbs were just like he had left them, so his horses had to be back in the brush somewhere.

The area wasn't big enough to lose two big horses, so he walked around the lake and into the trees. It only took a few minutes to find them standing three-legged in the shade, nose to tail, sleeping as horses do.

When they heard him coming through the brush, they raised their heads, looked in his direction, and went back to sleep.

"Well, boys, don't let me disturb your nap." He returned to his cave and ate venison and the last of his coffee. When this was gone, it would be a venison, jerky, and water diet.

He kept up the hot water bath several times a day. It seemed like it was doing some good. The left arm was not as sore, so he worked it a little at first, but the more he stretched and worked it, the better it felt. By the third day, it was almost as good as new. The right shoulder was still causing him lots of problems. There seemed to be some infection, and at times, a throbbing pain kept him from getting any rest. His day consisted of bathing his wounds, eating and sleeping, checking on his horses, and walking around the lake for exercise. But after almost a week, he was so bored he couldn't stand it any longer.

The best he could calculate was that he had been on the trail and hiding out for about ten days and was anxious to return to civilization.

The following day he was up early, brought the horses down to his cave, and very gently, mostly with his left hand and arm, got the saddle and packs loaded before stopping for a brief rest. The horses seemed as anxious to leave this place as he was, and when he stepped into the saddle, his horse broke into a fast trot straight to the trail they used coming up here. When they arrived at the trail-head, they stopped and waited while Jim removed the brush. When the path was clear, Jim had to mount with the horse already moving, and before he was firmly seated, they were on the steep incline to the river below.

The trail consisted of many sharp drops of several feet, which the horse didn't hesitate to jump right into. Jim was unprepared for his shoulder's shock and almost passed out from the pain. If there had been room for the horse to turn around, he probably would have reconsidered leaving until his shoulder had healed some more. But since turning around was not an option, he braced himself and took the rest of the trip without too much pain.

The pack horse was following behind without being led. When they reached the river and turned south, both horses stopped, took a deep breath, rested their legs for a couple of minutes before taking to the water, and slowly found their way along the river bottom. The water was clear and only a couple of feet deep in most places, so they could pick their way around and over most obstacles.

They reached the mouth of the canyon and the valley that he had been looking at from above for the last week.

CHAPTER 13

Jim was so out of it with pain and fatigue when he came this way before that he didn't remember any landmarks, so he sat back and let his horse find its way. He only knew he should be going in a southwesterly direction, and that's where his horse was going.

Jim was very tired after only a couple of hours in the saddle, but he pushed on, anxious to get back and find out what happened after he left town with Robert in tow.

A few more hours and he had to stop and rest. His shoulder was hurting, and his lack of stamina from being laid up for so long was showing.

The trail they had been on for the last several hours was winding through the hills, up and down the hillsides, and crossing streams, so when he came to the next clear running water, he pulled his horses under a shade tree and dismounted. He loosened the cinch on the saddle and the pack saddle, and the horses went directly to the water and drank their fill while Jim stretched out in the shade with his hat over his face. He dozed and dreamed of Vicki and wondered what she had been doing in his absence. Did she even miss him at all? Was she worried about him? What did Robert tell her when he returned? He could imagine the story she got, and it didn't make him feel any better. Robert was not the type to tell the truth, but he was the type to tell a story to make Jim look as bad as possible and make Robert look like a hero. The more Jim thought about it, the madder he got. Pain shot through his shoulder as he pushed to a sitting position, reminding him he was in no condition to take on anyone in a fight. He would get killed in a fistfight and stand even less chance in a gunfight. A five-year-old could outdraw him. He had to devise a plan that wouldn't get him shot or hung.

The horses were going where they wanted to go with no guidance from Jim. But, knowing the way of horses, Jim assumed they were taking him back to the home place near Rogersville, where they grew up. That was their home and where they got their feed, so it would be natural for them to want to go back there. Or, maybe they were going back to Vicki's place since that's the last place they were stabled and fed. Jim's only hope was the trail they were on would take them through Hazard. He could ask for directions if he met someone who didn't want to shoot him for the bounty on his head.

The horses occasionally broke into a trot, causing considerable pain to his shoulder, and he had to pull them back to a walk. They plodded along until late evening when he started looking for a place to camp for the night. He didn't want to be too near the trail. He preferred no one know where he was until he was ready to let them know. First, he wanted to get to Vicki and let her know he was okay and make sure she had not suffered any harm from helping him. He didn't know what he could do about it if she did, considering he could barely feed himself.

Before it was too dark to see what he was doing, he rode off the trail into the brush and set up camp. He thought he was far enough off the trail to have a fire that no one would see. He slowly and carefully dismounted and loosened the cinch and tie-downs on the pack saddle. He didn't like leaving the saddle and pack on the horses overnight, but he had too much trouble getting them up there to go through that again. They would have to deal with it for one night. Maybe by tomorrow night, he would be at a town with a livery stable, and they could get a good feed and rest in a nice warm stall. Maybe he could find a nice comfortable bed. Just the thought of it made him smile.

He put together a small fire for comfort because he had nothing to cook and no coffee, which he dearly missed. He did love his coffee, just like his daddy. He could go all day without food if he had his coffee. All he had left were a few strips of jerky and a little of the smoked deer meat.

When his fire was down to nothing but a bed of coals, he rolled out his blankets and turned in for the night. It seemed like he only closed his eyes when his horses awakened him. He opened his eyes and looked as far as he could see without moving. When he didn't see the cause of the noise, he slowly rolled over and looked toward the horses. Both were standing with their heads up, ears pointed forward, looking toward the trail. He eased out of his blankets and stood by them with his hand on their nose to keep them quiet. Several times, they wanted to nicker, but he kept them quiet until they settled down. When he was sure there was no longer a threat, he returned to his blankets and was almost immediately asleep. As usual, it was a rough night. The ground was too hard and lumpy, and his shoulder still gave him trouble. He was glad when the sky started to get brighter and daylight was just around the corner. He sat up, took in his surroundings, and discovered they were just like he had left them last night. He stood up and stretched to try to get some of the tightness out of his body, but it didn't seem to do much good. He was stiff and sore all over.

There was nothing to do but roll his blankets, attach them to the pack saddle, cinch up the saddle, and pack and mount up. When he reached the trail, he saw the tracks of two horses that passed in the night headed in the same direction he was going. He wondered who would be out here in the middle of nowhere that late at night. It was none of his business, but with nothing else to occupy him, he kept an eye on the tracks as he rode. A mile or so farther along the tracks left the trail and went off into the brush. Jim stopped and looked off in that direction. The brush and trees were so thick he couldn't see very far, but the tracks continued. He wondered where they could be going. There was no road or trail where they turned off. Curious, he followed the tracks to see if he could add a piece to the puzzle. The brush and weeds were pushed down, leaving a clear trail. He had only gone a short distance when the ground dropped off into a valley. It looked like several thousand acres of open meadow with a stream flowing through it. He stopped to admire the view. A small herd of deer was feeding near the creek, and farther down, a black bear with two cubs was playing in the water. What a beautiful place for a homestead. There wasn't a cow or horse in sight, nor a house or barn. He wondered how that could be. A beautiful place like this, and no one lived here. He turned his horse back to the trail when he heard a cow bawl. He stopped and looked back but saw nothing. The cow didn't sound like it was very far away, but it sounded like it was stranded or in trouble. He rode farther out onto the open valley floor. The first thing he noticed was the fresh cow and horse tracks. They were in a bunch, not like cows grazing, but like they were driven. Farther along, he discovered fresh tracks of two horses herding the cows. Now, who drives cows at night? He answered the question; those who don't want to be seen. So, why would they not want to be seen? He answered his question again; that isn't their cows they are driving. He hesitated a few minutes and then followed the tracks. A hundred yards farther, he found the cow doing the bawling. She apparently had slipped away in the dark and was left behind when the rest of the herd was driven away. He noticed the brand on the left hip, but it meant nothing to him since he wasn't from these parts and didn't know any of the local brands, but he stowed it away in his memory bank for possible use later. Her udder was stretched tight, making him think she and her calf had gotten separated during the night, and she was not happy. He rode a wide circle around her and picked up the trail farther along. From the way horse and cow tracks tore up the ground, he was pretty sure the two men were having a hard time driving the cattle from their home grazing ground. He came upon another big old longhorn hiding in the brush a little farther along. She saw him before he saw her, and she was ready to charge until he put the spurs to his horse and raced on past her. It was apparent why the riders let that one slip away. She was too much trouble and was likely to get one of them hurt or killed, so they wisely let her go when she broke from the herd.

He stayed on their trail, and an hour later, it branched off onto another trail that looked like it had been used several times recently. The fresh tracks wiped out the older ones, but the old manure droppings were still plain to see. He thought this looked like a gang of rustlers was hitting the ranchers regularly.

Following the tracks was easy. It looked like they were making no effort to conceal their crime if that's what was happening here.

A short time later, their tracks dropped down a cliff into a canyon with a stream flowing through it. The cattle tracks and the horses of the men driving them disappeared into the water. The stream was approximately twenty feet wide with steep banks, so the cattle were forced to stay in the water. There was no way to tell if they went up or down the creek. After thinking about it for a few minutes, he decided the logical direction would be upstream since they had been traveling in that direction all day, or all night, in their case.

He was having second thoughts about following them up that narrow canyon. They could pick him off at will if he were caught in there. It would be like shooting ducks in a barrel. He wouldn't stand a chance.

He was still trying to decide if he wanted to follow their trail any further when the decision was made for him.

"Sit right there, fellow, and don't make a move. I got a rifle aimed right at your back. One wrong move, and it will be your last. Drop your pistol and rifle on the ground, and then you can turn around. I want to see what you look like."

Jim was shocked when he first heard the voice from behind him. He didn't move a muscle until the man stopped talking, and then he slowly lifted his pistol from the holster and leaned as far over as he could to let it drop to the ground. The rifle was a little harder to get to as it was on the right side of his saddle, so he had to reach over with his left hand, and that arm was still very sore, but he managed it without hurting himself too much. The rifle dropped to the ground, and he turned his horse around and saw a poorly dressed man of about nineteen or twenty years old standing behind a large bolder with a rifle pointed directly at him. His hair was dirty and hanging down past his collar, and a scraggly blond beard that was several months old only made him look worse.

"Howdy, what's the rifle for?" Jim asked, "Do I look like a bad guy?"

"Don't get smart with me, or I'll put a bullet between your eyes. Now shut up and get off that horse."

"What's the meaning of this? I've never seen you before, so what have you got against me?"

"Why are you following us?"

Jim got a puzzled look on his face, "I didn't know I was following anyone. I was looking for a place to camp for the night. I've been riding all day, and my horse is tired, and I'm tired. Put that rifle down, and we can talk about it."

"You've got about three seconds to get off that horse before I shoot you off."

"OK, keep your pants on; I'm getting off if that will make you happy." Inside, Jim was sweating bullets. He could tell this guy was nervous and might pull that trigger at any moment. He slowly lifted his leg over the back of his horse and lowered it to the ground. That put his horse between him and the guy with the gun. One of the handguns taken from the men he shot earlier was in the saddlebag right by his right shoulder. While his movements were hidden from the man's view, he swiftly raised the flap, lifted the six-shooter from the saddlebag, and slipped it in his belt behind his back. He didn't know if it was loaded or if a bullet was in the right place to do him any good, but this looked like his only chance. This guy was probably part of the gang that stole the cattle, and they didn't want anyone to know what they did with them.

Jim calmly walked from behind his horse and faced the young man.

"Okay, what do we do now?"

"You do exactly what I tell you."

"Okay, tell me something. What are we going to do now?"

"Shut up. I'll tell you what to do when I'm ready."

"Okay," Jim said, "I'll sit over here on this rock until you're ready."

Jim moved to the rock that was about knee-high and sat down. He never turned his back to the man and tried to appear relaxed and unconcerned. That seemed to make the guy even madder. He stammered and stuttered and didn't know what to do next.

He repeated his earlier question, "What are you doing following us?"

"Like I already told you, I wasn't following you; I was looking for a place to set up camp for the night. This creek looked like a good place with plenty of water and shade. Are you camped close by?"

"Shut up. I'll ask the questions."

"Okay, what do you want to know?"

"Nothing, just shut up and let me think."

Jim could tell this guy wasn't too bright, but he was nervous and might pull that trigger whether he intended to or not.

"How about you take your finger off that trigger before you shoot someone? You would really feel bad about that, and your mama would never forgive you."

"You leave my mama out of this. She don't know nothing about what I do."

"But I bet she's proud of the nice young man you've turned out to be. Don't you think so?"

"I told you to shut up. Don't talk about my ma."

"Okay, do you live around here?"

"I told you to shut up and let me think."

Jim sat quietly, watching for his chance. The young man was in a quandary, undecided about what to do next.

"My name is Jim Carter. What's yours?"

"I'm Rufus Weatherman."

"I'm glad to meet you, Rufus. How did you end up out here all alone?"

"I'm not alone. I have friends."

"Oh, where are your friends?"

"I'm not gonna tell you."

The sun was long gone behind the mountains, and it was getting dark fast.

"Look, Rufus, it's getting late, and I need to set up camp before it gets too dark to see." Jim stood and walked toward his horse. "Do you want to help me?"

"No, stop. Stay where you are."

The rifle was wavering back and forth, and Jim was afraid it would go off. He stopped and waited for Rufus to make the next move.

Before either could do anything, a man stepped from the rocks behind Rufus. "What's going on here, Rufus? What you got there?"

Rufus jumped like he was stuck with a hot poker and whirled around to see who was talking. "Wilbur, I was questioning this guy to see why he was following us."

Wilbur looked like an older version of Rufus, so Jim assumed they were brothers, with several years between, but Wilbur appeared to have all his marbles in the same bag. This could be big trouble. Wilbur was armed with a revolver on his hip and a rifle. He descended the trail from the cliff with his rifle aimed at Jim.

"Well, what did he tell you?"

"He ain't told me nothing except Ma is gonna be mad if I shoot him."

"Okay, Rufus, you go on back to camp. I'll talk to this gentleman, and don't worry about Ma. She won't know anything about shooting this man."

"You mean you're gonna shoot him? Can I watch?"

"No, Rufus, I'm not gonna shoot him. You go on now."

Rufus dropped his head disappointingly, turned back into the rocks, and disappeared.

When he was out of sight and hearing, Wilbur turned to Jim holding his rifle loosely in the crook of his elbow but pointed in Jim's direction. "Okay, were you following us or not?"

"No, I wasn't following anyone; I was looking for a suitable place to spend the night. This looked like as good a place as any. I was about to start a fire when Rufus popped up with his rifle and started asking questions."

"What are you doing this far off the trail? Are you hiding from the law?"

"Now, why would you think that?"

"Maybe you are the law. How about you empty your pockets? Dump everything on the ground."

Jim slowly reached into his pockets and pulled out a little change, a few matches, and a folding knife. He pulled a paper from his shirt pocket, thought better of it, and pushed it back in. Wilbur saw the move and asked, "What's that paper in your pocket there?"

Jim hesitated momentarily and said, "Oh, just a note I had; it's nothing."

Wilbur walked closer and held out his hand, "Let me see what nothing looks like."

Jim thought this might work to his advantage. If this guy really is a cattle thief, he can't go to the law and claim the reward. He slowly removed the wanted poster from his pocket and handed it to Wilbur.

He took one look and started laughing. "Well, well, look what we have here. Jim Carter is wanted for murder. The boys are gonna like this."

Wilbur was still looking at the poster and not paying attention to Jim, so he casually reached for the pistol tucked in the back of his belt. It slid into his hand with such ease that Jim pointed it directly at Wilbur when he looked up. His eyes got big, and he dropped the poster and tried to bring the rifle up, but before he could get a good grip on it, Jim said, "Drop the rifle."

Wilbur was stunned but froze and looked at Jim, "Where did you get that gun?"

"I've had it since before you got here. Your brother was a little too careless. I could have killed him and you anytime I wanted to. Are you gonna drop that rifle, or will I have to shoot you?"

Wilbur carefully laid the rifle on the ground.

"Now back up, sit on that rock, and don't make another move until I tell you."

Wilbur backed up and sat on a large rock about ten feet from his rifle. Jim carefully walked to the rifle, picked it up, dropped his pistol in the holster on his hip, and checked the rifle to ensure it was loaded and had a round in the barrel. It was ready to fire, so he walked around to where his pistol and rifle lay on the ground and picked them up. Without turning his back to Wilbur, he slid the rifle into the saddle holster and placed the pistol in his belt in front.

Wilbur noticed that Jim moved slowly and carefully with his right arm and shoulder. "What happened to your right arm?"

"Why do you ask?"

"The way you are moving makes me think you may have taken a bullet not too long ago."

"A couple of murderers tried to kill me."

"What happened to them?"

"I killed them."

"So, that explains the wanted poster."

"No, that was another matter. That fellow thought I would be an easy one to bully."

"So you killed him too?"

"They say I did. He was still alive when I left the bar."

Wilbur looked puzzled and asked, "But you did shoot him, right?"

"No, I hit him with my fist."

Wilbur looked at Jim with a whole new outlook. "Well, you must be a lot tougher than you look."

"Maybe I am. I'm gonna ride on out of here before some of your friends show up, and I have to kill somebody else."

Jim knew he would have trouble getting on his horse, so he led him over to the rock he had previously sat on, stepped upon it, and then into the saddle. "I'll leave your guns up the trail a piece. Don't be in too big of a hurry to get to them."

"Carter, we could use another good man in our operation. How about you join us?"

Jim looked at him and smiled, "No thanks, that's not my line of work."

"Okay, how about you forget you ever saw me, and I'll forget I ever saw you, fair enough?"

"Fair enough," as he turned his horse and, still pointing Wilbur's rifle at him, walked his horse and led the pack horse back the way he came. He looked over his shoulder and saw Wilbur sitting on the rock. When he reached the creek junction and the trail, he leaned the rifle against a tree and continued into the darkness.

CHAPTER 14

Jim and his horses were tired, but he had to keep moving until he found a place to throw down his bedroll for the night. He didn't want Wilbur and his gang disturbing his sleep.

He was nodding in the saddle and almost fell off when his horse took a jump down a sharp drop. Jim grabbed the saddle's horn and steadied himself while he looked around to see where he was. Everything was pitch black. The moon had not risen yet, so he couldn't see much. His horse was making his way down a steep slope bracing his feet and sliding as much as walking. He finally came to a stop and took a deep breath. "Well, boys, this looks as good a place as any. What do you say we stop here for the rest of the night?"

He didn't know what time it was, but he figured it must be close to midnight. He had been riding since early morning. He was so stiff he had difficulty keeping his balance when his feet hit the ground.

He started to remove the saddle but remembered how heavy it was and how it hurt when he tried to lift it, so he left it on the horse. "I hate to do this to you, boy, but I don't have any choice. I'll make it up to you when I can."

He loosened the cinch to make it a little more comfortable. There wasn't much he could do with the pack saddle. He had no idea what was around them, whether grass or water was nearby, so he hobbled both horses and threw his bedroll on the ground. Before he removed his boots and lay down, he poured water into his hat and gave each horse a drink. "I know that isn't much, but that's the best I can do now."

He placed the hobbles on the horses and, with his feet, pushed the rocks away until he had a place cleared large enough to spread his bedroll. There were still a few rocks that he had to move. It took a while, but he could rest comfortably without something poking him in the back and ribs.

He awake late the next morning and looked for his horses. Both were standing where he left them, looking very disgusted with him for leaving the saddle and pack on all night and nothing to eat or drink.

He sat up and looked around to see where he was. Pine trees and thick underbrush-covered cliffs rose several hundred feet above him. Not twenty feet from where he slept was a sharp drop-off. He slipped his boots on, walked to the edge, and looked down, took a few steps back, and chills when up and down his back. If he had taken another twenty steps in the dark last night, he would have plunged a hundred feet or more to his death.

When his heart settled down, he walked closer to the edge and looked down again. A small stream flowed between the steep walls, making him look upstream. About one hundred yards away was a waterfall of about a hundred feet. There didn't appear to be any way to get to it from here. He did not need to go there, but it sure was pretty.

"Well, boys, we need to get moving. I know y'all are hungry and thirsty, and I could use something to eat myself." He removed the hobbles, tightened the cinch on the saddle and packs, and looked around for something to stand on to help him get in the saddle. A chunk of the wall had broken away, leaving a large pile of rock and dirt just the right size. He led his horse to it, stepped upon it and onto the saddle, and turned upstream. He didn't know where this would take him, but he didn't want to climb back up that steep embankment.

His horse picked his way through the boulders and debris along the edge of the cliff above the canyon. There was no trail, but the ledge was wide enough for a horse.

The sound of the waterfall got louder the closer he got. When he was close enough to get sprayed, he stopped to enjoy the view. From the top of the fall to the bottom was about three hundred feet, and it bounced off ledges and boulders on the way down. He could sit here all day and never get tired of the view, but he needed to move on, so he touched his heels to his horse and continued toward the fall.

A trail, probably made by deer, went up and around the fall to the higher elevation. Once he passed the waterfall, the terrain leveled out and made for easy traveling. The stream was about twenty feet wide and flowing fast, but it wasn't too deep, so when the game trail he was following crossed, he followed it and continued in a southwest direction, which he hoped was taking him closer to home and Vicki.

A surge of sadness shot through him when he realized he had no home. It had been taken away in the blink of an eye by those six dirty murderers. He had some satisfaction knowing he had killed five of them and realized he would have to settle for that. He was laid up for so long that he had no idea where the other one was.

He tried to figure out how long he had been gone, but couldn't come up with a reasonable number, so he gave up on that.

He finally came out on a well-used trail, or road, heading in the right direction, and followed it the rest of the day.

Just before sundown, he was looking for a place to stop for the night when he spotted smoke. There wasn't enough for a forest fire but too much for a campfire, so he assumed there must be a town ahead.

When he got close enough to see the lights from the town, it was almost too dark to see anything else, but he continued until he came to the first building, which looked like a livery stable with a lantern hanging over the large double door in front.

He had gone so long without a shave and haircut that he wouldn't recognize himself if he met him on the street, so he took a chance and rode up to the door and dismounted.

A booming voice came from inside, "Hello there, stranger. What can I do for you?"

"Do you have room for a couple of horses for the night?"

"I sure do. Bring 'em on in. Just park 'em over there and leave 'em. I'll remove the tack, give 'em a good rubdown and a big scoop of corn. They look like they could use it."

Before he led them inside, they dragged him to the watering trough and drank their fill. They seemed to know they would get a good meal when they went through the door and wasted no time going straight to a stall and checking the feed box. There was nothing there, and both looked around like they were accusing him of neglect.

The man with the booming voice had a body to match. He stood well over six feet and must weigh close to three hundred pounds. Some might think he was fat, but they would be mighty wrong. His arms were larger than most men's legs, his chest and shoulders bulged with muscle, and his stomach was flat, with no bulge.

Jim took one look and thought, *"Now, there is one heck of a big man. I sure don't want to tangle with him."*

As Jim started to remove the saddle and pack, a massive hand on his shoulder stopped him, "Hold on there, young fellow. That's what you're paying me for."

"Okay, if you insist. Where can I get something to eat this time of night?"

"Dirty Gertie's diner is the best place to eat for miles, and don't let the name fool you. The food is good, and the service is better. I'm Bill Smith, but most people around here call me Tiny. I've never figured out why."

Jim laughed at his joke, walked to the big double doors, and looked out. Turning back to Tiny, he asked, "What is this place called?"

"This is Evanson."

"Who's your sheriff?" Jim asked.

"Oh, we don't have a sheriff. Never saw the need. Everybody looks out for each other, just like one big family."

"That's good. That's the way people should be. This would be a much better world if everybody treated their neighbors like that."

"You sure got that right young fellow. By the way, if you don't mind me asking, what's your name?"

"No, I don't mind at all. I'm Mike Butcher." That's the name Jim had decided to use until he got his clear. "Is there a hotel or boarding house where a man can get a good night's sleep?"

"I can't guarantee a good night's sleep, but Widow Monroe runs a clean boarding house and serves good food.

"That sounds like what I'm looking for. Where might I find this Widow Monroe?"

"She's straight down that street, the third house on the left."

"Great, how much to room and board these two horses for a night?"

"That'll be two bits each for the room and another nickel each for the board. That comes to sixty cents."

Jim handed over the sixty cents, took his saddle bags, rifle and bed-roll from his saddle, and said, "I'll see you tomorrow, Tiny."

He walked the short distance to the boarding house and was met at the door by a middle-aged woman who looked like she had had a rough life. Her hair was mostly gray, and deep wrinkles around her eyes and mouth showed the results of hard work, but she had a big smile when Jim asked about a room for the night.

"Yep, I sure do. Supper's on the table now and getting cold, so come on in and eat, and then we'll get you settled in your room. Just drop your things right there and come on in."

Jim did as he was told and walked into the dining room, where a long table took up most of the space. There were ten chairs around it, and all but two were occupied. He pulled out the closest one and sat. Before he could see who else was there, a cup of steaming hot coffee was placed before him. It smelled so good his hands were trembling when he picked it up and took a sip. "Ah, that's the best coffee I've tasted in a coons age." A couple of snickers came from around the table, and Jim looked up to see who else was there.

Most looked like local businessmen, but two looked like salesmen from how they dressed. One didn't fit in that caught Jim's attention and caused him to take a second look. The man was sitting directly across the table from him and was looking straight at him when Jim looked up. The man was wearing part of a worn-out confederate uniform, had long shaggy hair, and needed a shave. He looked like he had not bathed in quite some time, and his smell confirmed it.

Jim tried not to stare, but it was hard not to. That could be the man that killed his parents and burned his home. He was sure of it but needed more proof since he had not seen him up close. Jim didn't know if the man recognized him, but he wouldn't take any chances. He knew he wouldn't stand a chance in a face-to-face fight with fists or guns, so he had to play this smart. He forced his eyes back to his plate and began to eat. His heart was racing, and his mind was almost numb with hatred for this guy. He wanted to pull his gun and blast away, but too many people here could get hurt. He had to wait for a better time and place.

He was having a hard time keeping his eyes off the man. He continued to eat, but his mind wasn't on the food.

He had to see his horse to know if this was the man. If he rode the black with four white stockings, Jim would make him regret ever setting foot in Tennessee.

Jim's hands were shaking so bad he was having trouble eating. He watched the man out of the corner of his eye. It felt like he was staring at Jim constantly, but Jim kept his eyes on his plate and did his best to appear to ignore him.

If the man had a room in the boarding house, that would complicate matters. He would have to wait and see how things played out.

The man finished eating and was ready to leave the table, so Jim pushed his plate away and said, "That sure beats jerky and half-cooked rabbits any day of the week."

There were a couple of grunts of agreement from around the table, but no one commented.

Jim was stalling with the second cup of coffee to see what the suspected killer would do when he got up and walked out the front door. Jim waited until he had time to get on up the street, then walked to the door, keeping to one side so the man wouldn't see him if he looked back, and watched to see where he went. It was too dark to see much, but a few houses and stores, mostly saloons, with lights inside, let him see his man when he passed one of them.

When Jim thought it was safe to step outside without being seen, he pushed the door open and quickly stepped out into the dark. He stayed there until the man turned the corner onto Main Street and was out of sight. Jim left the porch and jogged to the corner. As he approached the last building, he slowed to a walk and peaked around the corner just in time to see the man look back over his shoulder and, not seeing anyone, dart into an alley and out of sight.

Jim was tempted to follow but realized a good way to get killed was to follow a wanted man into a dark alley.

He returned to the dining table where the other men were still eating or sitting around talking and drinking the last of their coffee.

"Do any of you know the fellow that just left?"

All eyes turned to him, but no one said anything. Jim waited for several heartbeats and repeated the question. A couple of the men looked at each other but said nothing.

"Okay, what's the deal? Either you know him, or you don't."

Finally, one of the men, who looked like he was maybe a local merchant, spoke up, "I don't know him, but he's been around town a few days and spends most of his time in the saloon. Don't spend much money but takes all his meals here. I don't know where he stays at night, but it's not here."

"Do you know what kind of horse he rides?"

"That I do know; he has a pretty black with four white stockings and a blaze face. A nice looking horse."

Jim was getting more excited with this news, "Do you know where he keeps him?"

The men looked at each other, shook their heads, and said, "Now, that's a good question. I saw him when he rode into town, but I ain't seen him since."

"How long has he been in town?" Jim asked.

"You're sure asking a lot of questions, fellow. What's your interest in this guy?"

Jim thought for a second, "It's a personal matter that we have to settle."

"That sounds like trouble. What has that fellow done?"

"As I said, it's personal, don't get involved." Jim turned away, picked up his rifle from where he had left it with his gear on the floor, and walked out the door. Before he got off the porch, he heard someone at the table say, "I wouldn't want to be in that other man's shoes. That young man looks like he has a bad mad on. I think I'll stay away from the saloon tonight."

Jim left the porch and jogged to the corner again. After looking to ensure no one was waiting for him, he sprinted across the street to the livery stable where his horses were, hoping to find a black horse. Knowing the man had time to get back here and be waiting for him, he went through the door, darted to the side with his back to the wall, and waited. Nothing happened. After a few minutes, he took a chance, moved to the first stall, and waited some more. Still, nothing happened. He didn't know where Tiny lived, so he couldn't check with him, so he had to do this on his own.

After what seemed like a half hour, but probably wasn't more than ten minutes, he slowly walked the barn's length, checking the horses in each stall. His two were there enjoying the hay Tiny had thrown to them. Both looked up when Jim passed but gave no other sign that anything was out of order.

Jim completed the trip through the barn, checking all the stalls without finding the horse he was hunting. A large corral was attached to the back of the barn. Jim eased up to the edge of the barn's back door and looked outside. A dozen or so horses and mules milled undisturbed around the corral. Jim waited a couple of minutes until he was satisfied no one was around, and then he eased through the door and moved to the right, where he last saw his man.

CHAPTER 15

There were no lights anywhere, and everything was pitch black. The moon hadn't risen yet, and the few stars showing didn't do much good.

Since he knew the man hung out at the saloon, he would ask if they knew anything about him, like where he kept his horse.

He went back through the barn, onto the main street, and turned left toward the saloon. He took his time and stayed in the shadows as much as possible. When he approached an alley, he was extra careful, stopping and peaking around the corner before he continued. He made it to the saloon without incident, pushed through the bat wing doors, and up to the bar. A mirror on the wall behind the bar allowed him to see the entire room without turning his back to the bar.

The bartender came to take his order, wiping the bar with a semi-clean towel as he walked toward him. "What'll it be, fellow?"

Jim took a moment to answer. He had just spotted his man sitting alone at a corner table in the back facing the door.

"I'll have a beer, please."

"Ah, a polite one for a change. Your mama must have raised you right."

In a voice loud enough for everyone in the room to hear, he replied, "Yeah, she tried until some dirty scums killer her and burned the house down on her."

The room suddenly got quiet. The bartender said, "I'm sorry to hear that. When did that happen?"

"It must have been almost a month back. There were six. There's one left, and I intend to kill him before the night's over."

Jim watched the man at the back table as he spoke. His head was down, pretending not to pay attention to what was happening around him.

Jim took his beer in his right hand, and with his rifle in his left, holding it like a pistol, he moved down the bar. Everyone at the bar moved back out of his way and let him pass. When he reached the end of the bar about six feet from the killer, he stopped. The man still looked down at his drink on the table before him. Jim waited, staring at the man until he looked up.

"What are you looking at?"

Jim waited another full minute before answering. The man was nervous, looked around the room, glanced toward the back door, and back at Jim.

"You and your murdering friends killed my ma and pa and burned the place to the ground with them in it."

"I don't know what you're talking about; I've never been to Tennessee."

"Who said anything about Tennessee?" Jim asked.

"You did, you said...."

"No, you're the only one who mentioned Tennessee."

The man glanced toward the back door again.

"Don't even think about it. I'll cut you down before you get out of your chair. On second thought, go ahead since I'm gonna kill you anyway. It makes no difference to me how you get it."

The killer's eyes darted around the room as if he were looking for help, and sweat ran down his forehead into his eyes and dripped off his nose. He wanted to wipe it off but was afraid to make a move.

Jim waited some more, making the man sweat. Finally, he said, "Stand up and drop your gun belt to the floor. Feel free to try to shoot me any time you feel lucky. I hope you do. I've been waiting for this for a long time. I've already caught up with all your murdering friends, and now it's your turn."

The back door was flung open, and a girl, looking like a soiled dove, and a young man barged in, laughing and staggering as they forced their way between Jim and the killer. The man lunged for the back door, but the couple was between them, blocking Jim's line of fire. The man dashed for the door and was outside before Jim could get a clear shot. Jim cursed under his breath and darted out the door into total darkness. Coming from the lighted saloon, he had no night vision at all. Just as he was about to turn back inside, a shot was fired from fifty feet away, the bullet missing by a hair and buried into the door behind him. Jim ducked, fired three rapid shots at the gun flash, and dived to his right. He hit the ground and rolled and realized his mistake. His shoulder took the brunt of the fall, and pain shot through him. He thought he had been

shot again but realized it was the same wounded shoulder. He lay there until he got his breath and recovered from the pain. By then, he knew the man would be long gone. He didn't know where he kept his horse, so he had no place to start looking.

He slowly got to his feet and started back into the saloon. Just as he was pushing the door open, he heard someone moaning. He stopped to listen and heard it again. It came from the direction where the shot was fired at him. He pulled his pistol from the holster and moved to the side. He didn't want to walk directly upon the man if he was faking an injury. He circled to come in from the side. The closer he got, the more moaning he heard. His eyes were finally adjusting to the dim light, and he saw a man lying on his back, holding his chest. Jim cocked his pistol and spoke to the man, "Can you hear me?"

He heard a gasp and finally, "Yes."

"Okay, throw your gun over here."

"I can't, I'm shot, and I'm dying."

"Throw that gun over here, or I'll shoot you again."

"Okay, don't shoot."

Jim heard the gun hit the ground a few feet away, and with his revolver at full cock and aimed at the man, he moved in closer. It was too dark to make out much of anything, so he took a big chance getting this close.

Several people came from the saloon, neighboring houses, and businesses to see what the shooting was about.

"Can someone bring a light? This man has been shot."

Someone ran into the saloon and returned with a lantern. A man lay on the ground with blood on his shirt. It looked like the bullet hit him in the middle of his chest and came out his back.

Someone said something about getting a doctor, "Don't bother," Jim said, "This man is going to die one way or the other. If he doesn't die from the gunshot, he'll hang."

"What's he gonna hang for?" Someone asked.

Jim answered, "For murder and robbery."

"Who did he murder?" Another one asked.

"He murdered my ma and pa for two of them and several more during robberies over the last couple of weeks." Does anyone know where he keeps his horse while he's in town?"

"Have you checked the livery stable?"

"Yeah, it's not there," Jim answered.

Someone else asked, "What does his horse look like?"

Jim told them, "Black with four stockings and a blaze face."

Another man spoke up, "I saw one that looks like that in the corral behind that old abandoned shack at the west end of town. You might check that out. It ain't been used in years."

"Thanks, I'll do that."

While they talked, the man twitched a few times, gasped for breath, and was silent. Jim went through his pockets and found a wad of cash which he showed to the curious bystanders. "This money was stolen from a town south of here. I'm going that way, so I'll return it to them."

He peeled off a five-dollar bill and gave it to one of the spectators, "That should take care of his burial. Does anyone have any questions before I leave?"

No one said anything, so he walked away feeling empty now that the search was over and all six of the gang were dead.

It was too dark to go searching for the man's horse, and he knew the boarding house would be closed for the night, and he had left before he got a room there anyway. He went to the livery stable, retrieved his bedroll from his saddle, found an empty stall, and went to bed.

After a restless night, he awoke almost as tired as when he went to bed. He lay there thinking about the past several weeks and wondering what he would do now. He had no home or family to return to, two beautiful girls he had taken a strong liking to, and a reward on his head for murder.

When he thought of the reward, he sat up and looked around to see if anyone was watching him. All was quiet until he heard Tiny's booming voice say, "Well, I thought you were gonna sleep all day. You've already missed breakfast and are about to miss your dinner."

Jim stretched and rubbed his eyes, "What time is it?"

"It's half-past seven in the morning."

After a few minutes, he asked, "Do you think Widow Monroe is still serving breakfast?"

"If you hurry over there, she will probably take pity on you and give you something to eat."

Jim stood up, stretched again, straightened his clothes as best he could, tried to get all the hay off, and walked to the boarding house to see if he could get breakfast.

Mrs. Monroe was cleaning up after her boarders had eaten and left for their day jobs. When Jim came in, she gave him a look that reminded him of his ma when he went to the table after everyone else had eaten.

"I'm sorry, Mrs. Monroe; I had a rough night and overslept this morning. I'll settle for a cup of coffee if it's not too much trouble."

"Don't be silly. No man ever left my table without a full belly. Sit down. I'll have it right out."

Jim was the only one at the table, and Mrs. Monroe was in a talkative mood, "Did you hear about the shooting last night? Two men got in a gunfight over some floozy at the saloon, and one of them was killed. What is this world coming to? It seems like there's a killing every week or so. It's all that drinking and loose women that's doin' it. I swear there ought to be a law against it."

Jim decided to play ignorant and not get into the conversation. She continued to rant and never gave him a chance to respond. He was just as content to leave it like that. He finished his breakfast as fast as possible, asked where his gear was, retrieved it from the corner of the entry hall, paid her for his breakfast, and left before she brought up something else.

He returned to the livery to saddle his horses and get on the trail to....where? He still had a murder charge hanging over his head, and Vicki was waiting for him to return. Or was she? She probably had forgotten all about him since she hadn't heard from him in several weeks. He got a sinking feeling in his gut. That would be his first stop when he left here.

He brought his horses out of their stalls and began preparing them for the trail.

"Hey, Tiny, do you know how far it is to Surgoinsville?"

"No, never heard of it. Where is that at?"

"It's south, in Tennessee."

"No, got no idea. Why do you want to know that?"

Jim thought for a moment before answering, "I've some friends down there. I thought I'd drop in for a visit. How far is it to the Tennessee line?" Tiny scratched his head, thought for a moment, and said, "You ought to be able to make it in a couple of days if you don't lollygag none." With all his gear packed on his horses, he paid Tiny what he owed him, said his goodbye, led his horses out of the barn, and stepped into the saddle.

Then he remembered the killer's horse that may be in that abandoned barn on the edge of town. It was right on his way out of town, so he stopped when he reached the barn and looked inside. Sure enough, he was there looking like he had not had water or food in a long time. All the man's gear was there, so Jim saddled the horse, led him to the nearest water trough, let him drink his fill, and then went back to the livery and asked Tiny if he would like to buy a good horse.

Tiny came out, looked him over, checked his feet and teeth, and wanted to know where he got him.

Jim told how he came by the horse and had no use for him, but he was too good of a horse to turn loose. "I would like to keep him, but I don't want to be reminded of where he came from every time I look at him."

"I understand that. What do you want for him?"

"I'll take fifty dollars and give you a bill of sale."

Tiny agreed, handed over the money, and Jim left town.

Both horses picked up the pace when he turned south, knowing they were going home. He let them choose their pace for the first fifteen minutes, then pulled them back to a comfortable speed that he knew they could maintain all day, with an occasional stop to let them catch their breath and a drink of water.

Just before sundown, on the second day of his trip, he unexpectedly came upon a small town that looked familiar. He rode a little farther and realized this was where Vicki lived, and that was her house on the right.

He pulled his horses to a halt and reviewed what he remembered from when he was here. The first thing that came to mind after realizing Vicki was near was that Robert was probably here and carrying a grudge. He would have to be very careful to avoid him.

He rode off the road and came in the back way to get to the barn. He rode into the barn, dismounted, dropped the reins, knowing the horses would stay here, and proceeded to the door at the front end where he could see the house. All was quiet, which was to be expected this time of the day. He thought about going to the cafe to see her, but the place was probably full of people eating an early supper, so he abandoned that idea and decided to wait until she came home.

He removed the saddle and pack, led both horses into stalls, and gave each a scoop of oats. He threw his bedroll on a pile of hay in the corner and stretched out to rest.

He struggled to stay awake for the first half hour, but then he said what the hey, laid his head back, and drifted off to sleep.

It seemed as if he had just dozed off when a noise from nearby awakened him. He lay perfectly still until he identified where it was coming from and what the noise was. It sounded like two or three people arguing, and it was coming from the house.

He quietly rose from his bed of hay and made his way to the end of the barn closest to the house. From there, the voices were loud and clear.

"I've told you before, Robert, I am not interested in anything you have to say, so just leave and stop bothering me."

"You can play hard to get all you want, but you belong to me, and the sooner you realize that the better off you'll be. I'm not taking no for an answer, so don't make me get rough."

"Robert, get out of here," that was Vicki's mother putting her foot down.

"You stay out of this. This is between Vicki and me."

Jim had heard all he needed to hear. He lifted his pistol from the holster and stepped through the door behind Robert, but Vicki and her mom saw him when he pulled the screen door open and stepped inside, "Well, Robert, still up to your usual trouble-making, I see."

Robert whirled around and saw Jim standing four feet away with a gun in his hand. His face turned red and white while he stuttered and stammered, trying to say something but nothing came out.

"What's the matter, Robert? Cat got your tongue?"

Robert finally managed, "Where did you come from?"

Jim smiled and said, "Oh, I've been around. Vicki and her mom have both told you to leave, now I'm telling you to leave, and if you ever show your face around here again, I'll finish what I started a while back. Now get out of here."

Robert was pale and shaking as if he was looking at a ghost, "Alright, I'm leaving, but you ain't seen the last of me."

"I guess that's up to you, but if you come around here bothering Vicki and her mom again, I'll permanently put an end to you."

Robert slowly backed out the door and down the steps. As soon as his feet hit the ground, he took off running. Before he was out of sight, Vicki was in Jim's arms, kissing all over his face and crying and laughing simultaneously. "I've been so worried. Where have you been?"

He held her tight, accepting her kisses and smiling. When he could talk, he said, "I've been laying up in the hills, taking a break, enjoying the scenery."

"How are your wounds? Do they still bother you?"

"Just a little if I put too much strain on them, especially my shoulder. It isn't completely healed yet."

Vickie's mom stepped up and hugged him, "I'm glad you're back, but you better watch out for Robert; he's just foolish enough to try something stupid."

"I'm afraid you're right. I'll keep my eyes open when I'm around here."

Vicki asked, "Did you find those men you were looking for?"

"Yep, found every one of them."

She waited for an explanation, but when none came, she asked, "Well, what happened?"

Jim hesitated, not wanting to go into the details of the killings, "Let's just say they won't bother anyone else."

"Oh." Vicki's hand covered her mouth, and her eyes got big.

Then she asked, "What about the wanted posters? Have you been able to clear your name of that murder charge?"

"No, I haven't had time to get into that yet, but that's next on my list. Has anyone been around here asking questions or causing y'all any problems?"

"No, there have been a few strangers in and out of town, but nothing pointed to you, I don't think."

Jim was thankful for that news, "Maybe things have quieted down enough that I can start looking into what happened after I left that bar that night."

Vicki and her mom fixed a nice supper and sat around the table enjoying themselves. But before they sat to eat, they made sure all the doors were closed, and the curtains were drawn to prevent anyone from shooting them through an open window while they ate.

Jim explained, "Tomorrow morning, I'll head on down to Surgoinsville to talk with the sheriff who put out those posters."

"Isn't that dangerous?" Vicki's mom asked, "I mean, if he posted the reward, he's the one you should avoid at all costs."

"You're probably right, but I don't know where else to get the answers."

"How long do you think you'll be gone?" Vicki asked.

"I don't know. It depends on what I find out and what I need to do to fix it."

He rode out of town before the sun was up and reached Bristol on the border of Virginia and Tennessee just as the sun was setting. He had plenty of supplies to last until he reached Surgoinsville, so he skirted the town on the south side and continued until he found a place to camp and settled in for the night.

He figured to reach Surgoinsville sometime tomorrow. He had no plan for what he would do when he got there, but he knew that was where he had to start to clear his name.

His mind wandered when he settled into his blankets before falling asleep. He thought his best chance of having a meaningful life would be in Texas with his brother Ed and his brother-in-law Clay Wade. If he could convince Vicki to go with him, he would do that. Maybe he could convince her mom to sell the diner and go with them. That would make Vicki's decision much easier. Then the thought hit him; maybe neither of them would want to go anywhere with him. Perhaps he was setting himself up for a big letdown.

But first, he had to resolve this murder rap thing, and he didn't know how he would do that.

He was on the road before the sun was up the next morning. The horses sensed they were getting closer to home and kept up a good pace all day. They were as anxious to get home as Jim was. Except Jim knew there was no home waiting for him.

It took longer than he anticipated to reach Surgoinsville, so he had to spend an extra night sleeping on the ground and arrived on the outskirts about noon.

He knew he was taking a big risk, but his best chance of finding out what happened was to talk to the sheriff. But he had to plan things just right and pick the time and place to his advantage.

His hair was long and hanging to his shoulders, and a thick beard covered his face, so he looked nothing like he did when he passed through here several weeks ago.

Sitting on the edge of town, looking down the main street, he saw several people out and about, but overall everything looked quiet and peaceful. He studied the town for a few more minutes and then slowly rode down the street until he came to a livery stable. Assuming he would be here long enough for his horses to get a good meal and some well-deserved rest, he pulled up to the big double doors in front and dismounted. The keeper of the barn and the blacksmith came to the door wiping his hands on a dirty rag, "What can I do for you, Sonny?"

"I need to put my horses up for a while and give them a good feed. I don't know how long I'm gonna be here, not too long, I hope."

The man looked him over before asking, "You have business in town or are looking for somebody?"

"Well, kind of both." Jim answered, "Maybe you can give me some information to help me know where to start."

"I'll try; what do you want to know?"

"First off, I need to talk to the sheriff. Do you know where I might find him?"

The blacksmith looked up toward the sun, squinted his eyes, determined the time of day, and said, "My guess is he's probably in his office, sleeping. That's what he does about this time every day."

"That sounds like the kind of job I would like to have."

"Yeah, it would be nice, but most of us have to work for a living."

"You got that right." Jim remarked, "Does he have a deputy, or does he sleep alone?"

Laughing, he said, "No, he sleeps alone. I don't know anyone in bad enough shape to sleep with him anyway."

"Do you know a cowpoke by the name of Tim Watson? Jim asked, I used to ride with him a few years back. I think this is where he said he was from."

The blacksmith looked at Jim closer before he answered, "Yeah, I knew Tim."

Jim asked, "Is he still around?"

"No, Tim got himself killed a few weeks back?"

"Oh, I'm sorry to hear that. How did that happen?"

"I don't know how well you knew Tim, but he was a hothead, especially when he had a few drinks. He started trouble with a man smaller than him, a man about your size. He thought he would be easy to bully, but the smaller man was too much for him. Tim never laid a hand on him before this other fellow put him on the floor."

"You sound like you saw what happened."

"I did. I was sittin' not over fifteen feet away and saw the whole thing."

"What happened then?"

"Well, the little fellow, looking a lot like you, left the saloon, and Tim's buddies picked him up and sat him at the table, but he looked like he was having trouble gettin' it all back together, and a few minutes later he keeled over dead."

"Just like that, do they know what caused it?"

"The Doc said he probably had a heart attack from too much to drink and too much excitement. You see, nobody ever put Tim down before. He thought he was some tough nut to crack."

"So what happened then?" Jim asked.

"Well, this little fellow left town, but when Tim's daddy heard about what happened to his boy, he came storming into town and made the sheriff put out wanted posters on the fellow. I think his name is Jim Carter." The big blacksmith was giving Jim curious looks as he was telling his story, and Jim got a strong impression that he knew who Jim was.

"So, do you think this Carter fellow is guilty of murder?"

"No, I think Tim Watson bit off more than he could chew."

"Did you tell the sheriff that and Mr. Watson?"

"Yeah, we told both of them, but Watson wasn't having any of it. He wants your...that fellow's neck in a noose."

"How did the sheriff feel about hanging a murder charge on this fellow?" Jim asked.

"He was happy as a lark. He'll do anything Watson says. I don't know their arrangement, but something is going on there that many locals would like to know the answer to."

"I guess I'll walk over and talk with the sheriff. By the way, what is his name?"

"Miller, Cyrus Miller. I think he's some kin to Watson, but I don't know the connection. You be careful, young fellow. That man can be real sneaky at times."

"Thanks, I'll do that."

CHAPTER 16

Jim left the livery and walked down the street until he came to the building with the sign over the door proclaiming it to be the sheriff's office. Before he pushed the door open, he turned his right side to the door so no one would see him pull his pistol from the holster. The door opened easily without making a noise. Jim stepped in and closed the door. The sheriff was leaning back in his chair with his head resting on the wall, his feet on the desk, snoring away. On the desk was a nameplate, "Sheriff Cyrus Miller." His gun belt and gun hung on the wall behind him, so Jim eased over, removed the pistol from the holster, silently removed all the cartridges, and returned it to the holster. While doing that, he noticed the holster and gun belt were custom-made with fancy stitching and artwork. It was obviously made by someone who knew how to work with leather. That was an expensive rig, and Jim wondered how a small-town sheriff could afford such luxuries.

Jim looked out the window to see if anyone was interested in what was happening over there, but apparently, no one was concerned. He silently locked the door and pulled the shade over the window. The coffee pot was sitting on the potbellied stove. Jim eased over, touched it, and found it cold, so he sat in the chair in front of the sheriff's desk. The sheriff still hadn't moved except to snore. Once in a while, he jerked, sputtered, and snored again. He looked to be in his early forties, clean-shaven, and much better dressed than your usual small-town sheriff. His boots were hand-made with fancy stitching. Apparently made by the same person who made the gun belt and holster, and the hat hanging on the wall behind him was not your standard cow country hat.

It was hard to tell with him sitting the way he was, but Jim guessed him to be six feet tall and weighing around two hundred pounds. He didn't appear to have any excess weight, which surprised Jim. Maybe he had some outside activity keeping him trim, but that was not Jim's concern.

The door behind the sheriff's desk led to the cells in the back. Jim poked his head through the door and saw two empty cells with doors standing open. He then eased back to the front door, silently opened it, and closed it harder than necessary. The sheriff jumped, struggled to get his feet on the floor, and almost tipped his chair over. When his feet finally hit the floor, he sat staring at Jim for a few seconds before he asked, "What do you want?"

Jim pulled the wanted poster from his pocket, unfolded it, and dropped it on the desk. The sheriff took one look, his eyes got big, and he swallowed twice before saying anything. Finally, he said, "So you're the guy that killed Tim Watson?"

"No, I'm the guy you're accusing of killing Watson. Watson got himself killed when he attacked me that night. I understand all the witnesses told you it was self-defense, and Watson started the fight. So why are you so anxious to charge me with his murder?"

"Look, smart mouth, this is my town, I'll charge you with whatever I want to charge you with, and I'll see you stand trial and hang for his murder. How do you like that?"

"Look, Sheriff, I came here to talk to you man to man and find out why you are doing this."

"I'm doing it because you killed a man in my town."

"I already told you, and all the men who were there and saw what happened told you I was defending myself. So what's the real reason?"

"The real reason is that I don't like you."

"How can you not like me? You've never seen me before."

"I don't like anyone who kills someone in my town."

Jim sat thinking a moment and asked, "Who is Tom Watson?"

"Tom Watson is the boy's pa, and he wants his son's murderer caught, tried, and hanged."

"Does Tom Watson always get what he wants?"

"Tom Watson owns the biggest spread around here and packs a lot of weight when he wants to."

"So, how much is Watson paying you to do his dirty work, Sheriff?" Jim asked.

"Why, you mealy mouth no-good murderer." He sprang from his chair, grabbed the pistol from the holster hanging on the wall behind him, thumbed the hammer back, and pointed it at Jim. Jim calmly sat in his chair, watching the sheriff, who was stunned that Jim was still sitting there so relaxed as if nothing was happening.

"Stand up and drop that gun belt, and then you can march right into my jail cell."

"I don't think so, Sheriff, and it sickens me even to call you a sheriff. You are a disgrace to the law profession."

"GET UP!" The sheriff yelled.

"Okay, if that's what you want." Jim slowly stood and calmly drew his revolver from the holster. Sheriff Miller pulled the trigger on his pistol, but the gun didn't fire. He attempted to shoot Jim several more times while Jim pulled his pistol and cocked the hammer. "What's the problem, Sheriff? Your gun not working? I removed your bullets while you were sleeping on the job. Now it's your turn to go into your jail cell. Pick a cell, and you can sleep there until I decide what to do with you."

"Why you sneaky murderer. I'll get you for this if it's the last thing I ever do."

"Yeah, yeah, I'm shaking in my boots. Now get up and move, or I'll have to get rough with you. And as you know, I already have a murder charge against me, so I have nothing to lose. I can only hang once."

Sheriff Miller slowly backed away, looked at the gun in his hand, threw it across the room, and walked into the jail cell. Jim followed him and locked the cell door. "You rest easy there, Sheriff. If I think about it, I'll bring you something to eat when I get back."

"Where are you going?"

"I thought I'd ride out and talk with Tom Watson." Miller smiled and said, "I'd sure like to see that. He'll hang your hide from the nearest tree."

"You'd like to see that would you? Maybe we can make that happen. Do you have someone who can carry a message to him, asking him to come and see you?"

"Mr. Watson don't come when someone calls him. They go to him."

"Well, not this time. You're gonna write a note telling him it's urgent, he needs to come to town immediately, and then you will get someone to take it to him. Do you know how to do that?"

"Oh, yeah, I'm gonna enjoy this."

Jim searched through the sheriff's desk until he found a paper and pencil, handed it through the bars, and told Sheriff Miller to write.

Miller scribbled something on the paper, folded it, and stuck it in his pocket. "Andy Jackson will take it out to him."

"Who is Andy Jackson?"

"He's a kid about town who does odd jobs to make a little extra money."

"How do I find him?"

"He usually hangs out around the stage station and post office."

"Okay, give me the note." Jim said.

"You get him over here, and I'll give him the note."

"You must think I'm stupid to let you send that note without me reading it. Give it to me."

"Write your own note."

"Okay, I will, you may not like what it says, but you had your chance."

Jim sat at the desk and composed a note to Tom Watson, folded it, placed it in an envelope, and sealed it.

"I'll see you later, SHERIFF."

He picked up his hat and placed it on his head, took the cell's keys off the wall, put them in his pocket, and walked out the door. Down the street, at the stage station, he asked for Andy Jackson. A tall skinny kid who looked to be about fourteen years old jumped up from the bale of hay where he was sitting, "I'm Andy Jackson."

"Hi, Andy; Sheriff Miller asked me to find you and ask you to run this out to Mr. Watson. He acted like it was important. Can you do that?"

"Sure can. What should I tell him?"

"Nothing, just give him the note and hightail it back here, okay?"

"Sure, it'll take me a minute to get my horse."

Jim asked, "How long will it take you to make the trip?"

"It'll take about an hour out and an hour back."

Jim reached into his pocket, pulled out a quarter, and flipped it to Andy, who caught it in midair.

"Gee, thanks, mister."

Jim waited until he saw Andy gallop out of town heading northwest, then he strolled to the saloon where the fight took place. He wanted to talk with the bartender serving the drinks that night.

Since it was midday, no one was there except the bartender. He was sweeping the floor and putting the chairs and tables back where they belonged when Jim pushed his way through the bat-wing doors and up to the bar.

"Morning stranger, what brings you out so early?"

"Morning Sam, you wouldn't happen to have a pot of coffee brewing back there, would you?"

"Yeah, I just made it. How do you like it?"

"Black is good for me. Care to join me?"

"I don't mind if I do. What's on your mind? I know you didn't come here just for coffee."

"You don't recognize me, do you?"

Sam looked him over before answering, "You look familiar, but I don't know why. Have you been in here before?"

Jim took a sip of his coffee and looked around the room to be sure no one else was there, "Yeah, I was here the night Tim Watson got himself killed."

Sam looked around, assured himself that no one else was there, and said, "Yeah, I remember you now. You're taking a big chance coming back here. Don't you know there's a reward out for you? They're claiming you murdered him."

"Yeah, I know, that's why I'm here. I'm trying to find out what happened after I left."

"Well, after you left, Tim sat on the floor a few more minutes, like he was trying to make up his mind what he wanted to do, but he didn't look like he even knew where he was. The two men with him finally picked him up and sat him in a chair at the table with them. He seemed to be coming around, even talking some, said he would kill you if he ever saw you again, and then suddenly fell over on the floor. He was dead when I walked around the bar and got to him."

"I guess by that time, I was already out of town. Who started the talk about me killing him?" Jim asked.

"That didn't start until Tom Watson came into town and heard what happened."

"So Tom Watson is the one who brought up filing murder charges against me?"

"Yeah, he was the first one to mention it. We all tried explaining to him how the fight started and what happened, but he wasn't having any part of that. His mind was made up, and he told anyone who tried to talk him out of it to get out of his sight and tend to his own business."

Jim took another sip of his coffee, pushed his hat to the back of his head, and said, "And the sheriff went along with whatever Watson said."

"He always does. It's like Watson is holding something over Miller's head that makes him do anything Watson tells him to do, no questions asked."

Jim sipped his coffee and thought for a few minutes before speaking again. "I've sent word for Watson to come to town to meet with the sheriff. Do you think he'll come alone, or will he have a whole gang with him?"

"He won't come alone; he'll have that Mexican gunslinger with him. He never goes anywhere without him."

"Well, that puts a whole new light on the subject."

"What do you mean?" Sam asked.

"I was hoping to talk with Watson alone, but I guess I'll have to change my plans."

Sam got a concerned look on his face, "You're not thinking of doing something stupid, are you?"

"No, I just want to talk to him alone."

Sam shook his head, "Well, if you are dead set on doing that, you better have a gun in your hand. That Mexican gunslinger will shoot you down without blinking an eye."

"Thanks for the warning," Jim said.

He hung around drinking coffee and talking to Sam until the two hours were almost up, and then he went back to the sheriff's office. When he walked in, Sheriff Miller was fuming mad. "When are you gonna come to your senses and let me out of here?"

"Oh, I don't know, Sheriff. I remember what you said you would do to me when you got me in that cell. I'm tempted to take your advice and do the same thing to you. How would you like that?"

"I'm gonna kill you for this if Tom Watson doesn't beat me to it."

"I hear he's kin of yours, is that right?"

"Yes, and blood is thicker than water, and when he gets here, he'll teach you a lesson."

"We'll see about that, won't we?"

Jim left the jail cell and closed the door between the cells and the front office. He went to the gun rack on the wall, pulled down a double-barreled twelve-gauge, checked the loads, and saw the gun was empty. He took a box of shells from the shelf beside the gun rack, removed two shells, dropped one in each barrel, and snapped it closed. He then took several more, slipped them into his pocket, and sat beside the window where he could see the street. The shade was open a couple of inches to allow him to see out without being seen from outside.

Almost two hours after Andy Jackson left town, he came trotting back and went directly to the sheriff's office.

Jim saw him coming and unlocked the door before he got to it.

Andy pushed the door open, stepped in, and looked around for the sheriff. When he didn't see him, he asked, "Where is Sheriff Miller?"

"He had to step out for a few minutes. He asked me to wait here for you. Do you have a message from Mr. Watson?"

"No, he wasn't there, so I left the note with one of his men. He said he would get it to him as soon as he returned."

Jim thought a moment before asking, "Did the man have any idea when that might be?"

"No, and he didn't seem too anxious for him to get back any time soon."

"Okay, Andy, I'll tell Sheriff Miller when he returns."

Andy left, and Jim sat down to think about what he should do now that he may have several hours to wait. After a few minutes of thought, he came up with an idea that he thought would work better than sitting around here waiting.

He went to the cafe and asked if he could get a sack of sandwiches to take with him. With those in hand, he went to the livery, saddled his horse, and pack horse. The liveryman gave him directions to the Watson ranch, but he had no intention of riding into the headquarters and getting shot before he could plead his case.

He rode until he came to a rocky knoll with a view for several hundred yards up the road. When he was satisfied this was a good spot, he rode his horses a hundred yards off the road, tied them in the shade of a big pine tree, and returned to the road. He found a comfortable seat leaning back against a tree trunk and prepared for a long wait. He had no idea how long that might be, but from what he had learned about Watson, he didn't think the man would jump and run to the sheriff's beck and call.

He could see a half mile up the trail to where it dipped down behind a hill and out of sight, but farther along, he saw where it came up the other side of the next hill and over the top, so if he saw them when they came over that far hill, he would have about fifteen minutes or so before they got to him. That would give him plenty of time to see how many men Watson had with him, and if he needed to change his plan, he could still do it.

CHAPTER 17

I t was nice to sit back and relax for a while, but he couldn't be comfortable knowing that in a few minutes, someone could be killed, and it was all because of him. He could ride away from all of this, go to Texas, and start a new life, but his conscience wouldn't let him do that. He had to give this one last try. If it didn't work out, he could still leave, but he strongly felt that Watson was not the kind to forgive and live and let live.

The waiting became boring, but he had nothing else to do, and he saw this as his last chance to clear his name. So he pulled his hat down over his eyes and dozed. Every few minutes, he raised his hat and looked up the trail, but nothing was in sight.

The day was warm, with a slight breeze that made it feel just right. He became sleepier and his periods of dozing became longer.

He got up and walked around to stay awake while staying out of sight of the road. The sun was approaching the top of the hills to the west when he finally saw movement on the road on the far ridge. He watched a few minutes and determined four horsemen were coming his way. He suddenly realized they could be anyone. He had no idea what Tom Watson looked like. He may be about to confront the wrong man. What would he do then?

He didn't know, but he would figure out something, hopefully, before they got here.

He checked his pistol, rifle, and shotgun for the fifth or sixth time and saw they were fully loaded. He went over what he would do, where the men would be on the road, and what he expected them to do. He expected the sight of the shotgun would put a damper on anything they might think of doing, but he was worried about that Mexican gunman. You could never depend on what someone like that would do. But he could only do what he could do. His mind was made up, and it was too late to turn back now....or was it? No, he could still change his mind. All he had to do was let them ride on by, but then he thought about what Watson had already put him through and what the future held if he didn't stop it here.

He watched until they went out of sight behind the hill, and then he stood and stretched to get the kinks out before he had to do whatever he had to do. He stepped behind the big pine, out of sight of anyone approaching from their direction. He held the shotgun and leaned his rifle against the tree in easy reach. He peaked around the tree to see if he could recognize Watson in the group. If one of them was Watson, it would be the big man riding out front like a general. The horse was a big, long-legged, high-stepping brown. If Jim had to guess, he would say it was a Tennessee walker, but he didn't care. He just wanted this finished.

The closer they got, and the better he could see their features, he thought the big man looked a lot like he remembered Tim Watson looking.

That was the man causing him all the trouble. He felt a slow mad building inside. By the time they were even with him, he was ready to shoot Watson out of the saddle without warning, but he couldn't do that.

He wanted Watson to see his face and know the pain and suffering his son had caused.

He forced himself to calm down and wait. The horse's hooves struck the hard-packed surface of the road. There was no talk coming from the group. It was like they were riding on a grave mission and didn't want anything to distract them.

Jim smiled when he had that thought, "Boy, are they gonna be distracted."

The man he assumed was Watson was riding out front with the Mexican gunman on his right rear. That put Watson closest to Jim, which was ideal because it put Watson and one of the other men between Jim and the Mexican gunslinger.

Jim waited until they were even with him before he stepped out with the shotgun pointed at Watson and demanded they stop.

"Hold it right there, Watson, don't anyone move until I tell you, or Watson gets a full load of buckshot."

"Woo, what's this all about?" Watson said as he pulled his horse to a stop in the middle of the road, "Don't anybody do anything stupid. Let's hear the man out before we kill him."

"If there's gonna' be any killing here today, I'll do it, starting with you. All of you, one at a time, drop your gun belts in the road on the far side of your horse. Then dismount, starting with the gunslinger on the right. Drop your gun on the ground, now."

While Jim was giving orders, he walked to the middle of the road in front of Watson's horse, where he had a better view of all the men. He still had the shotgun pointed at Watson, but he watched the other men for any sign that they might make their final move.

The gunslinger sat still as a rock, never moving a muscle staring at Jim. Jim stared back until Watson finally spoke up, "Do what he says, Garcia. I don't think this man will kill anyone if you all do as he says."

"I don't want to kill anyone, but you have about five seconds to get those guns on the ground before I blow you out of the saddle."

Slowly the man unbuckled his gun belt and lowered it to the ground on the off side of his horse.

"That was real good, now get off the horse and walk back up the road."

Garcia took his time, deliberately going through the motion as slowly as possible.

Jim waited him out with the shotgun still pointed at Watson. When his feet were on the ground, he stood beside his horse and refused to move.

Jim waited a few seconds, "Get moving, Garcia, unless you want to see your boss get a load of buckshot in the gut."

Watson looked around at Garcia and told him to do what the man said. Garcia slowly walked up the road about ten yards, stopped, and turned around.

"Keep going. I didn't tell you to stop."

Reluctantly he turned and slowly walked up the road. When he had gone another ten yards, Jim turned to the next man in line and said, "Okay, you're next. Drop the gun."

When they were all dismounted and walking away, Jim turned to Watson, "Okay, it's your turn."

Watson didn't hesitate but dropped his gun on the ground and dismounted. "Now what?"

"Walk over to that rock and have a seat. We're gonna talk about Tim Watson."

"What do you know about Tim?"

"My name is Jim Carter, does that ring a bell?"

Watson came to his feet and started to charge Jim, but the shotgun in his face stopped him cold.

"Sit down; we're not through talking yet."

"You murdering son of a..... I'm gonna kill you and feed your body to the hogs."

"Now see, that's what I want to talk to you about. Why are you so dead set on killing me when several people have already told you that Tim started the fight and I was just defending myself? You have to know him better than I do, and you know he was a hothead and a troublemaker when he was drinking. That night he had way too much to drink, and when I came in, he thought he had an easy victim and would have some fun at my expense. All I did was protect myself from a beating. You, or anyone else, would have done the same thing. I don't know why or how he died, but he was still alive when I left the saloon. I'm told he got up, sat in a chair, and was talking with the men with him when he fell out of the chair and died. Isn't that the same story you heard from the men who saw everything?"

"I don't care what they said. I'm gonna see you dead if it's the last thing I do."

Jim heard a noise from up the road. When he turned to see what was happening, three horsemen were talking to Watson's four men. The horsemen pulled their rifles from the saddle scabbards, put the spurs to their horses, and came charging straight at him.

Jim lifted the shotgun and fired one barrel, knowing they were still out of range, but he wanted to stop their charge or, at the least, slow it down before they got too close. Just as he pulled the trigger on the shotgun, Watson barreled into him and knocked him to the ground. He dropped the gun, was on his feet in a flash, and cracked Watson on the head, stunning him long enough for Jim to grab the rifle from where he had left it by the tree. By that time, the three riders were only fifty feet away and firing at him as fast as they could pull the trigger with no regard for their boss, who was only a few feet away. Jim, standing behind the tree as he was, none of the shots hit him, but the tree would be dead if it were a man.

Jim poked his rifle and head around the tree and opened fire at twenty feet. There was not much chance of missing at that range. Three shots and three men were blown out of their saddles. The horses shied away from the gunshots and ran on past. One clipped Watson with a shoulder and sent him rolling. Jim rushed into the road, retrieved the shotgun, broke it open, replaced the spent shell, and snapped it shut. The four men up the trail ran toward him as fast as they could but were still two hundred feet away when he lifted his rifle and fired three quick shots into the ground. They slid to a stop and dived into the trees on the side of the road.

Jim looked back at Watson, who was getting to his feet and trying to brush the road dust off his clothes.

"Okay, Watson, you had your chance. This is your last warning. If I see any of your men or anyone who even looks like they may be your men, I'm gonna shoot on sight. I'm not gonna stand idly by and be shot or hanged for something your hotheaded kid did. Call off your dogs now, or you will likely be the next one who gets killed."

With that warning, he fired the two loads of buckshot in the ground at the horses' feet to get them started running. Fortunately for him, they ran toward town and not back toward the men. He then faded into the brush and was gone. His horses were where he had left them, so he stepped into the saddle and slowly rode into the hills doing his best to hide his trail. The ground was rocky and rugged and didn't leave much sign, but a good tracker wouldn't have any trouble following him. He had both horses and all his gear with him, so there was no need to go back into town. He took to the hills and rode until it was too dark to see, found a level piece of ground, and made a fireless camp for the night.

Before morning he was shivering from the cold and pulling for all the cover he could find. After several minutes of shivering, he got up and moved around. Maybe that would create some heat in his body. He stood up, wrapped the blanket around his shoulder, and checked on his horses. They had eaten everything within reach and stood looking at him. Now that it was light enough to see his surroundings, he was surprised to see he was in a wide open space in plain sight of anyone within a hundred yards. Last night it was so dark he couldn't see anything and was just looking for a place to crash for the rest of the night. When he saw how exposed he was, he grabbed his saddle, threw it on his horse, got the pack on the second horse, and was gone in a few minutes.

In the distance, he saw a piece of ground standing higher than most. He gradually worked his way to the top, and just before it leveled out, he stopped in a thick patch of trees surrounded by underbrush. He was a couple of hundred feet above the surrounding country and had a good view for many miles back the way he came. He decided this would be a good place to wait to see if he was followed. He loosened the cinches on the saddle and packs, took his rifle, and settled down under the low-hanging limbs of a poplar tree. The branches reach almost to the ground making a perfect hiding place. He could see the surrounding area, but he was hidden from anything over a couple of hundred feet away as long as he didn't move.

He had his canteen full of water and a small bag of jerky and could make out for the entire day if he decided to do so.

He sat back against the tree with his blanket wrapped around his shoulders and rested. He didn't know when he would get another chance, so he intended to take full advantage of this opportunity.

The sun came out and started warming things some, but he was back deep in the shade, so it didn't help him much yet, but he knew the day could get uncomfortably warm before nightfall.

After a while, he was nice and warm and starting to doze off and on. His head would drop and wake him up. He checked his back trail and still saw nothing. He crawled from his hiding place, stretched, and walked around to get the kinks out of his legs and back.

His horses were hidden well back in the brush below him. He gave each a drink of water from his canteen, talked to them, and petted them for a few minutes.

There was nothing for them to eat in this thick brush, so he knew he would have to move before nightfall and find a place where they had water and grass.

After a few more minutes, he returned to his previous lookout position. He had no more than settled down when he saw movement along his back trail at the far edge of his line of sight. He slowly picked up his rifle and ensured a round was in the barrel and ready to fire. He pulled his knees up, making a rest for his elbow to steady his rifle. He sighted down the barrel but couldn't make out what was there. He waited. That was always the hardest part, waiting. Time seemed to stand still in situations like this. He waited. Whatever it was approached a small opening about two hundred yards away. Too far to be sure of making a good hit, so he waited.

Was he going to shoot a man from ambush without giving any warning? He had already given them plenty of warnings. If that was Watson or his men, he didn't owe them any more notice, but he still couldn't bring himself to kill a man like that. He was a very good rifle shot, so if he got the opportunity, he could put the bullet where he wanted it. He had won several shooting contests back home, so he decided to take them out of the fight without killing them. If he killed one, the rest of them would keep coming, but if he wounded one, it would probably take two to get him to a doctor. That would temporarily take at least two, and maybe three, out of the fight.

He had good concealment and a good field of fire, so he waited for just the right time and place.

He didn't have to wait long. They were coming along at a slow walk, searching for tracks. Every so often, the lead man would point to the trail and say something to the men behind him. That was the man he would take out first since he was obviously the best tracker.

He sat perfectly still except for following them within his rifle sights. When they were about one hundred yards out, they would be in a small clearing with nothing between them and Jim. He would take the tracker first; if he had time, he would go for the Mexican gunman riding second in line. Jim had his sight on that open spot, and was ready when the tracker reached it. Still, he waited until the men following him were in the open, and sighted in on the man's right shoulder, took a very fine bead, squeezed the trigger, levered another round, and fired at the Mexican gunman. He didn't have as much time to be sure of his aim, but he was sure he made a hit just the same. Both men tumbled from their saddles and the other two scattered into the brush.

Jim waited, hoping the smoke from his rifle didn't give away his position. If they spotted him here, he didn't have enough cover to protect a rabbit. They could riddle him with bullets before he could do anything about it. He should have given more thought to that and waited in a place where he could withdraw without being seen. He was trapped here with nowhere to go. He was cussing himself for not thinking of that. If he survived this round, he would not let that happen again. That came from inexperience and never being in a situation like this before.

The two men still lay where they fell, but he saw both moving, so they were not dead. The other two still had not shown themselves since they disappeared into the trees and brush.

He was afraid to move a muscle. All he could do was wait for them to show themselves. Since no one had fired a shot at him, he was convinced they didn't know where he was; otherwise, they would have shot him to pieces by now.

All of this started about mid-afternoon, and now the sun was almost to the top of the mountains to the west. It would be dark in a couple more hours. Then what would happen?

After waiting a few more minutes, he had an idea that might work. He cupped his hands around his mouth and shouted, "Hey, you men down there. If you want to come and get your wounded, come on, I won't shoot."

There was silence for a few minutes, and then one of them shouted back, "how do we know we can trust you not to shoot?"

"I give you my word. I won't shoot."

He heard them talking, and one of the wounded men appeared to have answered. Jim thought he heard him say, "if he wanted to kill us, he would have already done it."

"Alright, I'm coming out."

Jim didn't answer. The man slowly came out of the trees and walked toward the two wounded men like he was expecting a bullet any second.

He went to each man, examined his wounds, determined they could ride, and called for his partner to bring the horses.

Jim watched while they loaded the men and started to ride away.

Jim called to them, "Tell Watson not to send anyone else after me. They won't be so lucky."

They slowly rode away back the way they came. Jim waited until they were gone before moving from his hiding place.

He went to his horses, tightened the cinches, and headed north. He was going north when he left Watson on the road and rode into the hills. He continued in that direction until he found a good camping spot with plenty of grass and water. He knew he wouldn't have to worry about anyone on his trail for at least twenty-four hours, so with a fire going, the coffee hot, he sat back and enjoyed the sandwiches he had brought from town. He didn't realize how hungry he was until he took that first bite. "Oh man, that's good." He was ready for anything with a sip of hot black coffee. He drank two cups and ate two sandwiches. By then, it was dark, the stars and moon were bright, and the night was quiet. After a few more minutes of relaxing and looking up at the sky, he pulled the sticks out of the fire to let it die down, rolled up in his blankets with his head on his saddle, and slept. Early the next morning he was on his way to Rogersville to see Sheriff Campbell. With a little luck he would soon be free of that murder charge.

CHAPTER 18

Watson's men arrived in Surgoinsville in the early hours of the following day. It was still dark and cold. They had been riding all night. They had to take it slow with two wounded men and tired horses. They went straight to the doctor's office and got him out of bed. He wasn't in a very good mood, but being a doctor, he was used to being awakened at all hours of the night.

He opened the door in his nightshirt with a ragged cap on his bald head while trying to get his spectacles in place.

When he saw two men holding two other men, he opened the door and stepped out of the way, "Bring 'em on in here. Put one in here and the other over there. Who seems to be hurt the worst?"

"They are both shot in the right shoulder, Doc. Neither looks too serious, but they need doctorin', so we brought 'em straight to you."

"How did this happen?"

"We were tracking that killer that murdered Tim, and he ambushed us. He almost killed all of us. If he were a better shot, these two would be dead."

The doctor cut the shirts off, examined the wounds, and saw that the bullets went through and out the back. He told the other two men to go on about their business and leave these two here for a few hours. "Let them rest and get some sleep." He cleaned the wounds inside and out, stitched up the holes, and applied clean bandages.

The day before, about sundown, Watson rode into town alone and went straight to the sheriff's office. He stormed in the door and looked around; no one was there, so he stormed out, went to the saloon, and stomped up to the bar.

"What'll it be, Mr. Watson, the usual?"

"Yeah, have you seen Sheriff Miller?"

"No, I haven't seen him all day. Did you check his office?"

"He's not there."

"It's about time for supper. Maybe he's at the boarding house, where he usually eats."

"Thanks, I'll check that out."

He downed his whiskey in one gulp, threw a quarter on the bar, and stormed out.

When he didn't find Miller there, he stood outside thinking where Miller might be and then decided to recheck his office.

Watson stomped through the door and yelled Miller's name. He heard an answer from the cell block, pushed the door open, and looked in, expecting to see some drunk. Instead, he found Sheriff Miller, red in the face, standing at the bars looking out.

"What are you doing in there?"

"That damn Jim Carter held a gun on me and forced me in here. What took you so long to get here? I expected you hours ago?"

"I would have been here earlier, but that "damn Jim Carter" held me up on the road, ran my horse off, and left me afoot."

"What happened to him?"

"Nothing, I've got men out looking for him. He'll never get away. I'll hound him until he's dead, one way or another."

Sheriff Miller shook the bars and said, "Get me out of here."

Watson went back to the front office to get the key. He returned a moment later and asked, "Where's the key?"

"It's hanging on the wall behind my desk where it always hangs."

"No, it's not. I looked there."

"Well, look on the desk. Maybe he...dammit, that Carter must have taken it. Look around. It has to be here somewhere."

Watson searched the office and reported back that there was no key.

Miller slumped down on the bed in the cell. Watson asked, "Do you have another key?"

"No, that's the only one."

Watson was furious, and Miller was furious. Watson asked, "What kind of sheriff only has one key to his cells? What if someone locks you in your own jail? How do you expect to get out? Damn, if you're not as stupid as your sister. I'm sorry I ever married that woman."

"I am too, Tom. I wouldn't be in the mess if you didn't marry my sister."

"Well, enjoy your stay, Cyrus." Watson stormed out the door with Miller yelling after him.

Watson returned to the saloon and had another whiskey and then another. After the third one, he left, went to the blacksmith shop, told him to go down and cut the sheriff out of his jail, and then mounted his horse and rode home.

The following day he was finishing his breakfast when one of the men he had sent out after Carter rode up to the corral and dismounted. Watson jumped from his chair, threw the back door open, and yelled for the man to come.

When the man, Jim Hargraves, got within talking range, he asked, "Where are the rest of the men?"

"Well, Mr. Watson, Garcia, and Thompson are at the doctor's office getting bullet wounds patched up, and Jason is waiting to bring them home when the doctor lets them go."

"That's just fine and dandy. Where is this Carter fellow?"

"I don't know."

"What do you mean you don't know? He shot two of my men and walked away. What were you doing while this was going on?"

"He ambushed us, Mr. Watson. He shot from the trees. We never saw him. He shot Thompson first and then Garcia. Jason and I dived for cover to keep from getting shot too. We never could spot him. Finally, he told us to come to pick up our wounded and tell you not to send anyone else after him, so we picked up Garcia and Thompson and took them to the doctor. They are both shot in the shoulder, nothing serious, but they lost a lot of blood. Doc said they'll be fine."

"Get out of here!" Watson said and slammed the door.

He turned back, opened the door, and yelled, "Hargraves, hitch up a wagon and go pick up our men!"

"Yes, sir, Mr. Watson."

Watson stormed back into his house and slammed the door. "Damn, can't anybody do anything right?"

His wife came in from the back bedroom, "What's wrong now?"

"I sent four men out to find one man, and they can't even do that. Two of them got shot, and the other two ran."

"Who was shot?"

"My main man, Juan Garcia, the one I can always depend on to get things done."

"Well, I hope they killed him. I never did like that man. He just looks evil. I don't want him around me."

"I'm sure he doesn't want to be around you either."

"Oh, Tom, you're so adorable when you talk like that."

"Shut your mouth, woman, and go back to your room."

"Why Tom, that's the nicest thing you've said to me in a long time."

"You're pushing your luck, woman."

"What luck? My luck ran out the day I married you. It's been nothing but hell ever since."

Watson grabbed his hat off the peg on the wall and slammed the door on his way out.

A few minutes later, she heard him gallop away toward town. She laughed, poured a cup of coffee, and sat at the table looking across the vast acreage she inherited from her father when he died a few months before she married Tom Watson. Shortly after they married, and she saw the kind of man she married, she wondered if Watson had something to do with her father's untimely death. But, by then, she was pregnant with his son, and her life had been pure hell. Then the son grew up to be just like his father. He was just as likely to slap or push her out of his way as his father was because he had seen it happen so many times he thought that's how he was supposed to treat women.

When Watson reached the town, he went straight to the sheriff's office. The blacksmith was there repairing the lock that he had cut off. Miller was nowhere around, so he went to the boarding house and had breakfast. From there, he went to the saloon and found Sheriff Miller sitting over a cup of coffee, looking like he had been on a ten-day drunk. There was no one else in the place except Sam, the bartender, who was busy cleaning up from the night before.

"Well, Sheriff, don't you look chipper this morning? How was your night? Did you get a good night's sleep?"

"Get out of here and leave me alone, Tom. I'm in no mood to listen to you today."

"You better listen to me if you want to keep that badge. I want you to get a posse together and go after that Carter fellow. He shot up two of my men yesterday, and I want him caught, and I want him dead, and I don't care how you do it."

"Where do you think I'm gonna get a posse in this town? Everyone knows what happened. They all think Tim got what he deserved. Everybody for fifty miles around knows he was a bully; he has always been a bully since he was a kid."

"You get ready to ride. I'll send four of my men to help you. They'll have their orders. You just go along to make it official. Got that?"

"Yeah, I got it."

Watson's four men showed up around three in the afternoon. Two of them, Hargraves and Jason Roberts, were the same ones that were with Juan Garcia and Thompson when Jim shot them. Miller had been waiting for the last two hours and was not in a good mood. First, he didn't like riding in this heat, and at night it was too cold, the food was terrible, and the coffee was usually cold. Miller started grumbling before they were out of town, and it never stopped until finally, Nate Rogers, from Watson's ranch, told him to shut up. He was tired of hearing it.

Hargraves and Roberts led them to the spot where the shooting took place. They picked up Carter's tracks and followed them until it was too dark to see. They made camp and got an early start the next morning. They were a full day behind, so they saw no reason to rush things and tire out their horses. They figured tracking him down would take a long time, so they came prepared.

They followed the tracks north for about five miles, then turned west and slightly south.

Sheriff Miller called a halt for the noon lunch break. When he dismounted from his horse, he almost fell to the ground. His back and legs were hurting, and he was hungry and thirsty.

As they were lying around in the shade eating, Miller brought up the subject of Carter being from Rogersville just south of here. "I'll bet you a plug nickel that's where he's headed. He's goin' home. Let's go to Rogersville and wait for him; if he's not already there, he soon will be. It can't be more than about fifteen miles from here. What do y'all say?"

Nate Rogers, who seemed to be in charge of Watson's men, said, "That makes sense to me. It ought to be almost due south from here, shouldn't it?"

"That's the way I figure it," Miller said.

Watson's four men finished eating, got to their feet, stretched, and headed for their horses. Miller was still slowly chewing his jerky and sipping from his canteen, "What's your hurry, sit down. My butt hasn't stopped hurting yet."

Watson's men were working cowboys accustomed to working from can-see to can't-see six and seven days a week, while Miller was content to sit on his behind in his office or the saloon.

Rogers looked back over his shoulder, "If you're going with us, you better get moving." He said as they turned their horses and rode away. Miller was struggling to get to his feet, groaning and cussing Watson, "I'm gonna kill that sorry son-of-a....."

By the time he got mounted, the rest of the men were already out of sight. He galloped after them and finally caught up a mile along the way.

Four hours later, they reached the outskirts of Rogersville. Rogers stopped the group and sat looking down the main street. There wasn't much to see this late in the day. Lights showed from the windows of some houses and all the saloons along both sides of the street. The working people were home eating or already in bed after putting in a hard day. The only people on the street were those who had nothing else to do.

Rogers asked, "Does anyone know what his horses look like?"

Miller spoke up, "Yeah, he was riding a good-looking buckskin and leading another equally good-looking bay carrying his pack."

"Okay, let's wait until it's good and dark and look for his horses first. That should give us a pretty good idea of where to start looking."

They rode slowly up and down the street and didn't see any horses fitting that description, so they checked the livery stables and still didn't find them. They met at the first saloon on the north end of town, stepped up to the bar, and ordered beers all the way around. They stood with their backs to the bar, drinking while looking over the patrons. None of them paid attention to the five strangers who had just entered.

The bartender came back to freshen the beers. Rogers asked him, "Have you seen Jim Carter in here lately? We were supposed to meet him here."

"No, I ain't seen Jim in over a month. Not since someone killed his family and burned his place. He just up and disappeared. I heard he was looking for the men that did it."

"Okay, thanks."

They finished their beers, left the saloon, and stood outside, trying to decide what to do next.

Sheriff Miller said he would see if the sheriff was in and if he knew anything. He strolled off to Sheriff Campbell's office and found him closing up to go home for supper.

Miller walked up behind him and spoke, "Hello, Sheriff."

Campbell spun around with his hand on his gun to see a man standing only three feet away.

When Miller saw him spin around, ready to draw, he stepped back and threw his hands in the air.

"Hold on there, Sheriff, I'm Sheriff Miller from Surgoinsville. I need a brief word with you if you have a minute."

"Oh, Miller, yes, I've heard about you. What can I do for you?"

Miller held out his hand to shake Sheriff Campbell's hand. Campbell reluctantly shook the hand, but there was no friendliness in it.

Miller was waiting for Sheriff Campbell to open the door and invite him in, but that didn't happen. Campbell waited for Miller to state his business.

Miller cleared his throat and stated, "I'm looking for Jim Carter. I have an arrest warrant for him. He killed a man in my town a few weeks back. Has he been seen around here lately?"

"No, he hasn't, and if he had, I wouldn't tell you or anyone else. I've known that boy all his life. I would be surprised if he killed anybody, and if anyone says he murdered someone, I will call them a liar to their face."

"That's some harsh words coming from an officer of the law."

"As I said, I've known that boy all his life, and there's no way he murdered anyone. If he killed someone, I'm sure they deserved killing. Why don't you tell me what happened."

"I didn't see it, but all the witnesses said he got drunk, got in a fight in a bar, and killed one of the local citizens."

"How did he kill him, Sheriff? Did he shoot him, stab him, or was it a fair fist fight, man to man?"

Miller got a surprised look and wondered what Sheriff Campbell had heard.

"It sounds like I'm wasting my time talking to you. You're not gonna be any help. Thanks anyway."

As Miller turned to walk away, Campbell warned him, "Miller, don't start any trouble here. You don't have Watson to bail you out in MY town. Get on your horse and go home."

Miller met his posse in the saloon and told them the sheriff wasn't going to help, "We might as well move on."

"We came here to get Carter," Roberts said, "We'll wait around a day or so and give him time to get here."

They did not know that Carter had never lived in the town. His home was several miles out in the country. While they lounged around town, Jim visited his mom and dad's graves. He knew every inch of that property. He and his brother and sister played and worked all over it in their growing-up years. Now it was just him. He walked around the grounds, visited the graves, and talked to his parents. When it was almost too dark to see, he mounted his horse and rode to the pond with the waterfall where he was to have met Jenny on that fateful day. He pitched his bed-roll near the pond, gathered enough wood for a fire, made a pot of coffee, and warmed a can of beans. When he finished eating, he lay dreaming of what might have been. He awoke during the night shaking from the cold.

He sat up and looked around to see what had awakened him. The horses were standing on three legs and sleeping on their feet. Nothing was stirring, but he felt uneasy. Like he was watched or followed. He took his rifle, moved away from the horses into the brush surrounding the pond, and took a seat leaning against a tree.

After thirty minutes, nothing had moved, and the horses were not showing any sign of anything around, he returned to his fire, added a few small sticks, and stirred it to life. The night chill made him shiver, so he wrapped his blanket around his shoulder and sat hunched over his fire until he was warm again.

From the stars and moon's position, he figured it was still a couple of hours before dawn, but he knew he wouldn't get any more sleep. He was almost out of food, so he planned to ride into Rogersville, grab breakfast at the café and see Sheriff Campbell. Being a lifelong friend of the family, he may be able to get the wanted posters canceled and called in.

He packed up his gear, saddled his horse, and headed for town, then realized he would ride right by the Henry place, so he would take this opportunity to stop in and talk with Jenny. He was not looking forward to that conversation. He was going to tell her about Vicki and their plans for moving to Texas and was dreading her reaction but knew it was something he had to do.

The closer he got to her house, the worse he felt. He didn't know how he was going to do this, but it had to be done.

He stopped his horse on the ridge overlooking her house and sat for a long time, hating what he was doing. Finally, he sucked in a deep breath and put his horse in motion. When he could see the front of the house, Mr. Henry sat on the front porch smoking his pipe and drinking coffee.

When Jim rode up, he said, "Well, Jim, it's good to see you again. Get down and sit a spell. Tell me what you've been up to."

"Thank you, Mr. Henry, but I just stopped to see Jenny if she is around."

"Maybe you better get down and come in. I'll get you a cup." With that, he got up from his rocker and went inside. Jim dismounted and dropped the reins on the ground. He hadn't planned to be here very long, but things were looking like those plans might change.

He took the chair next to the rocker and waited for Mr. Henry to return with the coffee. He handed a cup to Jim and took his seat.

"What happened after you left here, Jim? We heard something about you being wanted for murder. What happened?"

Jim gave him the short version and ended by telling him he was on his way to see sheriff Campbell to see if he could help to get things straightened out. "All the witnesses told Watson exactly what happened, but he has his mind made up to see me hang, and there is no changing it."

While they talked, Jim kept looking around for Jenny, but she had not shown herself, and whenever Jim brought up her name, her father changed the subject. Jim was getting worried that something awful had happened to her. He finally had had enough of the cat and mouse game and came right out and asked, "Where is Jenny, Mr. Henry?"

Mr. Henry clouded up and looked down at his feet and then out across the yard, everywhere except at Jim.

"Jim, I don't know how to tell you this, so I'll just come right out with it. She ran off with some fancy-dressed dude that came through here and filled her head with stories of fancy clothes and ballroom dancing in New York and California. The next thing we knew, she was gone. She left a note on her bed and slipped out one night. We ain't heard from her since. That was over a week ago. I'm sorry, Jim."

Jim was shocked. He hung his head and could think of nothing to say. After a long silence, he said, "I'm sorry too, Mr. Henry." After another long pause, "I guess I'll be going. You take care now. Say hi to Mrs. Henry for me."

"I'll do that, Jim. You take care of yourself and stay in touch."

Jim rode away with deep sadness and relief. Relief that he didn't have to tell Jenny about Vicki, but sad for what Jenny had done and the heartache she was causing her parents.

Jim reached town just as things were beginning to get busy. He went first to the café and had the best meal he had had in so long he couldn't remember when.

The place was packed, and he knew most of the faces there. Some waved and spoke, but no one paid too much attention to another cowboy coming in.

He found a table with one empty chair in the back by the kitchen and asked the men sitting there if they would mind sharing their table.

They didn't mind and continued their conversation like he wasn't even there. They soon finished, told him to enjoy his meal, and left.

He was just finishing his breakfast and enjoying his coffee when Sheriff Campbell came in. Jim held up his hand and motioned for him to join him. The sheriff looked surprised to see him. He looked around the room like he was looking for someone, hurried over to Jim's table, sat down, leaned in close, and said, "That Sheriff Miller is here with several men looking for you. You gotta get out of here before they see you."

The timing couldn't have been better, or worse, depending on how you look at it, but Miller and his "posse" came in the door and looked around for an empty table. When they didn't see any place to sit, they turned around and left.

Sheriff Campbell's back was to the door, so he didn't see them, but Jim told him what happened when they were gone. "Did they see you?"

"I don't think so; at least they didn't act like it."

"Okay, if you've finished eating, go out the back door and get out of town quickly. I'll meet you down by the old fishing hole north of town. You do remember it, don't you?"

"I'm not one of your town boys, but I've been there a few times."

He went out the back door and had not gone twenty feet when two men he had never seen before stepped out of the brush, pointing guns at him. Before he could react, something crashed into the back of his head, and everything went black.

CHAPTER 19

Sometime later, he awoke with a throbbing head; his tongue felt like old shoe leather, and his eyes wouldn't focus. All he could see was the horse's feet and legs and the dirt of the road beneath them. That's when he realized he was tied across the back of a horse.

He turned his head and thought someone had hit him again when pain shot through him like a lightning bolt. He groaned, threw up everything he had eaten, and passed out again.

The next time he awoke, he was lying beside a small fire, and several men sat around drinking and talking. His head was throbbing with every heartbeat, and he felt like he was gonna throw up again. He tried to sit up and realized his hands were tied behind his back and his feet were tied together. He struggled to no avail. The men laughed and said, "Well, lookie here, our guest of honor is finally gonna join us."

"Why am I here? What are you doing?"

"You will be happy to know you will be the guest of honor at a necktie party that Mr. Watson is throwing in your honor."

He pushed with his elbows and legs and turned to see who was there. The only one he recognized was Sheriff Miller.

"Why you cheap excuse for a lawman. I should have known you were involved in this underhanded deal."

"Get him on his horse. We've wasted enough time."

His feet were untied, and he was lifted onto his horse, sitting upright this time, and then they were tied together beneath the horse. They rode until late afternoon when they came to a ranch house sitting back off the road with large trees surrounding the grounds with several large barns out back with corrals.

When they rode in, Miller dismounted at the front door and, without knocking, pushed it open and walked in unannounced. The rest of the men sat on their horses, waiting with Jim.

A few minutes later, Mr. Watson came out with a smile.

"Well, Mr. Carter, so nice of you to join us. Take him to the barn. I'll be out in a minute. I need to get something."

When they arrived in front of the big barn, his feet were released, and he was dragged to the ground and shoved up against the barn wall.

A few minutes later, Watson appeared with a bullwhip in his hands. He popped it a few times and smiled, "Welcome to the party, you murdering bastard. I'm sure gonna enjoy myself, and I'll make sure you don't."

And then he spoke to the man called Rogers, "Tie his hands in front and hang him from that beam up there."

Jim was jerked around and shoved up against the wall. His hands were being untied, and he was ready. When the last strand came loose, he unwound as fast as he could. He was stiff, and his movements were limited, from being tied up like a pig going to market for the last six or eight hours, but he felt like this was his last chance, so he put everything he could muster into it. He hit the first man in the face so hard that he collapsed at Jim's feet. Two more charged, and he punched at anything that came into view. They couldn't get behind him with his back to the wall, and he was aware enough to stay against it. They kept coming, and he kept punching. Several fell and got up, only to be knocked down again.

He had the satisfaction of feeling his thumb gouge into an eye and another crumpled to the ground when Jim kicked him on the side of his knee, causing it to crack and buckle. After a few minutes, his arms felt like they weighed fifty pounds, and he struggled to stay on his feet, gasping for breath and held up by the barn wall when someone fired a shot, and everyone stopped.

"That's enough. Stand out of the way." The whip popped again, and Watson stood before him, holding the bullwhip and smiling. "If he doesn't want to be tied, I'm okay with that. He can take it like he is." He drew the whip back, popped it again, and started swinging it again when another gun discharged. Everyone jerked around to see who fired that shot.

Mrs. Watson looked out the window when Jim was brought to the barn and dragged off his horse. She muttered, "That must be the young man accused of murdering Tim." She went to an old trunk sitting against the wall under a window, lifted the lid, reached in and pulled out an old Colt Dragon pistol, checked to make sure it was loaded and dropped it in the pocket of her dress. She hurried out the back door and headed for the barn. When she saw her husband ready to use the whip on the young man, she fired a shot in the air.

She stopped ten feet from the group, "Is this the man who murdered my son?" She asked.

One of the men standing by with a bloody nose and swollen eyes answered, "Yes, ma'am, he's the one."

She raised the pistol and ordered everyone to stand out of the way. She walked within a few feet of Jim and looked him in the eye, "Did you kill my son?"

"No, ma'am," Jim said, gasping for breath, "I was in a fight with him that he started. When I left the bar, he was fine. I don't know what happened after I left, but I didn't kill him."

She turned her back to Jim and looked at her husband, "Turn this man loose and let him go. That sounds just like something your son would do, and he died, so this man got blamed for his death, now turn him loose."

Watson was furious, "Are you out of your mind, woman? Get out of the way, or I will use this whip on you."

"That would be just like you, Thomas John, always the bully. That's why your son was the way he was and the reason he's dead now."

Watson drew the whip back, and Mrs. Watson raised the big pistol and shot him. Watson was so surprised he might have died from shock if the bullet had not blown a hole in his chest and out his back big enough to put your fist in. He stood for several seconds with his mouth open, looking at the blood seeping out of the hole in his chest, and then he slowly crumpled to the ground. Everyone else was in total shock and couldn't move.

Mrs. Watson looked around at the group while holding the smoking pistol, ready to shoot again if anyone made a wrong move.

"Does anyone have a problem with what happened here today? If you do, speak up." No one said anything. They were still in shock.

Mrs. Watson looked around at the group again, "Okay, I'm running this place now. Y'all will take your orders from me, or you'll move on. This was my place before I married that piece of garbage, and it's still mine. Does anyone have a problem with that?" As she looked each man in the eye.

No one answered so she turned to Sheriff Miller, "Cyrus, you and the men take him out and bury him somewhere. Then you are going into town and notify every law officer in the country that the reward for this man is canceled, and you will recall all those wanted posters you sent out. You got that, Cyrus?"

"Y yes, Ester."

"When you've done that, turn the stupid badge in, get your butt back out here, and make yourself useful. The rest of you get that piece of trash out of my sight, then either pack your stuff and get off the place or get back to work."

Two men picked Watson up and dragged him out of sight. Mrs. Watson turned back to Jim, who was still leaning against the barn wall and couldn't believe what he had just witnessed. "And you, young man, I'm sorry for what you have been through. I wish I could make it up to you, but I have no idea how to do that."

"Ma'am, you just did, and I'll be forever grateful. I'm sorry you killed him, but I'm sure glad you did if that makes sense."

"Are those your horses?"

"Yes, ma'am."

"Okay, you better be on your way before something else happens."

"Yes, ma'am, and thank you."

"You're welcome; I should have done that twenty-five years ago."

Jim mounted his horse, took the lead rope on the pack horse, and rode away. He didn't know which way to go when he reached the main road. He had been chasing outlaws and chased as an outlaw for so long that he felt lost.

He sat on his horse for a few minutes trying to decide when his horse decided for him. He turned south and headed toward home. Jim let him have his head for the first mile and then pulled him down to a fast walk. He rode another mile or so before he heard a group of horses galloping in his direction. He quickly spurred his horse into the brush on the roadside and out of sight. He could see the road from where he was, and the group came into view in a few seconds. The man leading the pack was Sheriff Campbell, who looked like he was on a killing mission. Before they reached him, Jim rode out to the side of the road and waited.

Sheriff Campbell saw him and jerked his horse to a halt. He stared at Jim for a full minute before asking, "What happened to you?"

That was the first time Jim realized he must look terrible. He looked down at his shirt front and saw it was ripped to shreds and coated in blood. His face felt like a horse had kicked him, his eyes were swollen, and his nose felt funny. He reached up and felt it. It was a little crooked, but he was breathing through it, so it must not be too bad.

He looked up at Sheriff Campbell and tried to smile, "Everything's fine, Sheriff. Why do you ask?"

"Because you look like the devil himself got ahold of you."

CHAPTER 20

When they reached Rogersville, he was so sore it hurt to breathe and getting off his horse hurt so bad he was tempted to stay on him.

The doctor checked him out and determined he had a broken nose but no broken ribs, which surprised Jim. He would have sworn they were all broken.

After almost a week of lying around Sheriff Campbell's jail recuperating, Jim was ready to start living again. He felt like a huge weight had been lifted off him. He could breathe and enjoy it and didn't feel like he had to be looking over his shoulder all the time.

Lying in bed had given him plenty of time to think about what he wanted to do with his life, and tomorrow he would put that plan in motion.

Most of the swelling was gone from his face, but there were still a few bruises on his body that were sore, but nothing that he couldn't deal with, so early the following day, he said goodbye to Sheriff Campbell and took to the road. His horses were rested and eager to be going again.

Three days later, he rode into Hazard and went straight to the clothing store for a new change of clothes, then to the barber shop for a bath, shave, and haircut. Next, he went to the cafe to see Vicki. When she saw him enter the door, she knew everything was okay. She smiled, waved, brought his coffee, kissed him on the lips in front of everyone, and whispered, "I love you."

He turned red from his neck to the top of his ears, but he whispered back, "I love you too."

They smiled at each other, and she hurried back to the kitchen.

He spent the rest of the day watching her hustle around the room, taking orders, cleaning tables, and serving food. She sat at his table every chance she got.

The sun was gone from the sky, and it was getting dark outside when the last customer left. The front door was locked, and she cleaned up, put chairs back in place, wiped down the tables, and got all the dirty dishes to the kitchen. Before she finished, her mom came from the kitchen and told her to go home. She would finish up and be along in a few minutes. Vicki thanked her, removed her apron, turned to Jim, and said, "Let's go."

They slowly walked hand in hand down the street toward Vicki's house. She wanted to know everything that had happened since she saw him last. He gave her the highlights but left out all the more gruesome details. But he told her the reward was canceled, and the wanted posters should all be out of circulation by now. She turned loose of his hand, slipped her arm around his waist, and hugged him. He put his arm around her shoulders and leaned down to kiss her forehead. "I feel like a new man, with no one looking for me to hang me or collect the bounty money. I can lie down at night without worrying about someone sneaking up on me while I sleep. You have no idea how good it feels."

"Well, if it feels any better for you than it does me, you must be feeling pretty darn good."

"I do, and now we can start planning our future. When do you want to get married?

She was quiet for so long Jim thought she was having second thoughts about getting married. He looked down at her, saw a big smile, and knew he was wrong. "Well,…" Jim felt something tug at his collar, and a split second later, they heard the shot. He grabbed Vicki, and they scrambled into the dark of the nearest alley between two buildings. Another shot was fired just as they reached the alley, but neither shot did any damage. Jim felt his collar and said, "That was close."

Vicki asked, "What's going on? Who is shooting at us?"

"I don't know." But after a few seconds of thought, he asked, "Has Robert been around causing trouble?"

"He's always around. I can't do anything or go anywhere without running into him. He hasn't caused trouble, but he's always there."

Several more shots were fired into the alley, but Jim knew they were shooting blind, hoping for a lucky shot. He saw the gun flash from across the street, drew his revolver, took careful aim, and fired three quick shots. He heard a commotion, then "damn, I'm hit. Let's get out of here."

Jim knew whoever he shot was not hurt too badly, but he turned to Vicki, took her hand, and said, "Let's go out the back way and get to your house."

They made it to her back door and inside. "Don't light any lamps; we don't want to give them anything to shoot at."

They had no more than gotten settled on the floor in the corner of the kitchen, out of reach of any shots, when the front door burst open. Jim aimed his pistol at the intruder when he heard a panicked voice screaming, "Vicki, where are you?"

Jim relaxed, and Vicki answered, "I'm here, Mom. Everything's okay, someone shot at us, but we're fine."

"Why are you in the dark?"

"We didn't want to give them anything to shoot at. Come join us over here. "

There was just enough moonlight coming through the windows to see Vicki and Jim huddled in the corner. She hurried over and sat on the floor, and hugged Vicki.

"What happened? Were those shots fired at you?"

"They were fired at me, Mrs. Simpson," Jim answered.

"But why? You said the reward is canceled."

"I know. Maybe this has nothing to do with the reward."

"What do you mean?"

"I think Robert Phillips may be the culprit behind this."

"But why?"

"Jealously."

"But Vicki has told him repeatedly that she wants nothing to do with him."

"I know." Jim said, "But I don't think that's what Robert wants to hear."

"So what are you going to do?" Mrs. Simpson asked.

"First, I'm going to go outside and wait for him if he decides to come here to cause more trouble."

Vicki grabbed him and said, "Jim, don't go out there. You might get shot."

"I'll be careful. Y'all stay here and stay down. If you want to go to bed, pull the mattresses onto the floor and sleep there. That will keep you below the windows, so you won't be hit if he starts shooting into the house. I'll be out there to stop it, and don't worry about me."

He slipped out the back door and around the corner of the house next to Mrs. Damouth's house and slowly made his way to the front corner next to the street. When he saw no one on the street, or sneaking around in the dark, he eased down behind a thick bush at the corner of the house and waited. From there, he could see up the street toward town. The Simpson's house was on the north end of town, so anyone coming would come from the south, and he would see them long before they got there.

The wait wasn't very long. A shadow of movement across the street caught his attention. It looked like someone was trying to stay in the shadows of the houses.

Jim watched as the shadows materialized into three men crouching and moving from house to house until they were directly across the street from him.

He was ready with his pistol if they should start shooting at the house.

They suddenly sprinted across the street and stopped only a few feet from where Jim was hidden.

One of the men whispers to the other two, "You go round back and cover the barn in case he's hiding there like he did last time I had him cornered. I'll check the back door." Jim thought the voice sounded like Robert, but now he was sure of it.

The one going to the back passed within three feet of Jim as he came around the corner. Jim silently stood, took two steps, and brought his pistol down on the man's head. He crumpled to the ground without a sound. Jim quickly stepped to the corner of the house to see where the other man was and saw him trying to open the front door. His back was toward Jim, so he quietly stepped up on the porch and knocked him out with the barrel of his pistol. That man also crumpled to the porch. Jim grabbed his feet, dragged him off the porch and around the corner, and dumped him with the first one, and then he ran to the back corner of the house just in time to see Robert trying to get the back door open. He was so busy working on the door that he didn't know Jim was there until he felt the cold steel of the barrel of the pistol pressed into his neck below his ear.

"Hello, Robert," Jim whispered just inches from his ear as he lifted the pistol from Robert's holster and stuck it behind his own belt.

"It's so nice of you to come calling. You saved me the trouble of hunting you down."

Robert froze and stammered, "W w what do you want?"

"I want you out of my life, Robert. How do you suggest I do that? I've told you, Vicki and her mom have told you, we don't want you around. It looks like I'm just going to have to kill you."

Jim took hold of Robert's collar and pulled him toward the edge of the porch, "Let's take a walk. I don't want to disturb the women."

"NO, DON'T KILL ME!" Robert screamed. "I'll leave you alone. I won't bother her again, I promise. Just don't kill me, please!"

"I don't trust you any farther than I can throw you. Start walking."

"NO!" he screamed and dropped to his knees.

Just then, the back door opened, and Mrs. Simpson and Vicki came out, "Jim, what's going on? Who is that?" Mrs. Simpson asked.

"This is our friend Robert. He and some of his friends were trying to break into your house. A couple of his friends are waiting out front that I need to check on."

He handed Robert's pistol to Mrs. Simpson and said, "If he moves, shoot him, he has caused too much trouble already."

Mrs. Simpson took the gun, pointed it at Robert, and lit into him, "What in the world is wrong with you, Robert? Vicki has told you over and over to leave her alone. Why do you keep pestering her?"

Robert was shaking and stammering and finally said, "She's mine. If I can't have her, nobody else will have her, she's mine, and she's always been mine."

When Jim arrived back in front, the two men were just beginning to come around, holding their heads and wondering what hit them.

"Alright, on your feet, and don't try anything funny, or I'll shoot you right here, get moving." As he prodded them to their feet, he heard a scream, a shot from the back of the house, and another shot.

He sprinted around the house with his gun in hand, ready to shoot, thinking that Robert had somehow gotten the gun away from Mrs. Simpson. But when he rounded the corner, she was standing with the weapon in both hands pointed at the ground in front of her, and Vicki and Robert were lying on the ground. Vicki had blood on the front of her dress and wasn't moving. Jim ran to her side and dropped to his knees beside her, "Vicki, Vicki, talk to me, talk to me." He was shaking her so hard that she finally said, "Okay, don't shake me to death. What do you want me to say?"

He hugged her to his chest and held her so tight she could hardly breathe. He then remembered the blood on her chest and suddenly let her go to look down at her bloody clothes, "Are you shot? What happened?"

"No, I'm fine." She was crying and trembling as she pulled him back down to her and held him tight.

"What happened?"

Mrs. Simpson was still holding the gun and staring at Robert lying on the ground with blood covering the front of his shirt.

Vicki was crying too hard to talk, Mrs. Simpson seemed to be in shock, and Jim wanted answers, but no one was talking.

"Vicki, Vicki, look at me." He pushed her away to see her better, "Vicki, are you hurt? Have you been shot?"

She shook her head "no" "He grabbed me and was dragging me away when Mom shot him. He still didn't turn me loose, so she shot him again, and he fell on top of me. Is he dead?"

"It sure looks like it. We need to check on your mom. She looks like she needs help."

They got to their feet and went to Mrs. Simpson, who was still staring at Robert as if she was expecting him to get up and cause more trouble. Jim took the gun from her, and Vicki led her into the house and seated her at the table. She looked up at Vicki, "Did I kill him?"

"It's okay, Mom. He won't bother us anymore."

A small crowd had gathered outside the back door asking the usual questions. Jim went out and told the story. Some men shook their heads, and one said, "I knew that boy was gonna cause trouble. He has never been right in the head."

Jim asked, "Does he have family here?"

"None that I know of. I don't even know where he's from. He's been hanging around here for the last couple of years, doing odd jobs, just enough to keep himself fed."

Jim reached into his pocket, brought out ten dollars, and handed it to the man, "This should take care of getting him buried. Will you see to that?"

The man looked at the money and smiled, "You darn tootin' I will. For ten dollars, I'll dig the grave myself." He turned to some of the men standing by and asked them for help getting the body to the undertaker.

Jim went back inside and saw that Mrs. Simpson and Vicki were much calmer.

"Who would like some coffee?" he asked. They both said they would, so he got the coffee pot and started to fill it with water when Mrs. Simpson took it from him and said, "I'll do that. You go sit with Vicki."

"Thank you, ma'am." He hugged her and went to sit at the table with Vicki.

They sat holding hands, and Vicki asked, "Why couldn't he just go away and leave me alone? None of this had to happen."

"Like one of the men outside said, Robert never was right in the head. So don't blame yourself or your mom for what happened. He brought it all on himself."

"I know, but it's still awful."

"It's over, so let's not talk about it anymore, okay."

CHAPTER 21

The next day, Robert was buried on boot hill in a plain wooden coffin. It was a sad ending for a life cut short. Only a few local people attended, which did not include Jim or the Simpsons. They wanted to put the whole sordid affair behind them as soon as possible.

Vicki and Jim had discussed their wedding plans, which included going to Texas. They asked Mrs. Simpson to join them, but she smiled and said she had other plans. When asked by Vicki what they were, she blushed and confessed that she would be getting married also. Mr. Alberts, who owned the largest saddle shop in the area, had been after her to marry him for the last couple of years, and now that Vicki was getting married and moving away, she had decided to take him up on his offer.

After much discussion, they decided on a double wedding the following Sunday at the Baptist church immediately after the Sunday service.

Everyone from miles around knew Vicki and her mother, so the church was packed to capacity with people wishing both of them the best.

When the plans were finalized, Jim had mailed a letter to his brother in Cuero, Texas, informing him of all the latest news and that he and his new wife would be joining them as soon as they could get there, and asked him to have a spot picked out for them to homestead.

He still had to make arrangements to sell the home place and the livestock, but he had someone in mind who would probably be interested.

After the wedding, they made the trip to Rogersville and checked into the hotel. The next day Jim went to the bank and talked to the owner, who confirmed Jim's suspicions. Yes, he would buy the place and the stock. They agreed on a price, and the papers were signed. A check was deposited into Jim's account, they shook hands, and the banker wished Jim and Vicki the best of everything in their new life.

The next stop ... Texas.

The End

If you enjoyed reading this book, please look up other books written by Art Clepper.

<u>BOOKS BY ART CLEPPER</u>

LONG TRAIL TO TEXAS

REVENGE TEXAS STYLE

THE LOST MAN

NEVER YOUR LADY